ARE YOU HUNGRY?

ARE YOU HUNGRY?

J.J. Colagrande

Jitney Books

#MADEINDADE

#MIAMIFULLTIME

EPIGRAPH

For I mean to roam and think and make great irons red-hot.

—Knut Hamsun

ARE YOU HUNGRY?

TABLE OF CONTENTS

PART ONE STORIES

LOOKING FOR MARGARITA
Las Vegas, Nevada, 1998

You know, David, the moment I stepped off the plane at McCarron and witnessed this beautiful busty blond in the Self-Help section of the airport bookstore, right then I knew Vegas wasn't my scene. Before reaching the exit door of the airport the slots took me for ten and I told myself, make a U-turn, Keith. Tell me.

Will I ever listen to myself?

That was a rhetorical question. You didn't have to answer.

Besides, Margarita said it all. Listen, Keith. Let's give it a try.

You know she only moved here a week ago. She called yesterday with the idea. I was in a great state of mind and body because I just finished teaching my yoga class.

No, not Bikram. I teach Ashtanga.

She called and said Los Angeles will still be there if it doesn't work. I miss you sooo much. And then she had the nerve to say, I love you, Keith. I can't believe she had the nerve to say that. I love you has a strong effect on me. How does it affect you, David?

I'm sure every character does have their secrets.

Well, I love you turns me into a cat that's grabbed by the fur of its neck. I'm powerless. I mean look at me. Love lured me into chasing this girl, a Los Angeles waitress mind you, for all I know a possible prostitute, my gal for only two months.

Yeah, this is all I brought, just an overnight bag.

Figured I'd buy things when needed.

I'm not a material person, man.

No, this wasn't planned.

We broke up. I let her go. Like you'd let a captured butterfly or dove free. I thought if things were meant to be then they were meant to be. I mean, if Margarita and me were meant to co-exist, it would happen, in this life, or the next one, or the next one. And if destiny disagreed, then oh, well, that's just the way. But now I'm giving up.

Because this town's nuts.

Way too many nut-jobs here. I've had a crazy day and I know this is not my scene. I'll admit it, man. When the cab dropped me off outside the Luxor, I felt excited about seeing Margarita. Tingles burst through my stomach like popcorn popping in a kettle. Risk, lust, love, intrigue, whatever you call it. The feels lured me inside of this pyramid. Wish you could buy that feeling. It'd feel easier because I'm out of here.

You really want to hear about it?

It's a long story. Do you have the time?

Five minutes in the King Tut's lounge?

Yes. I know the place. I'm leaving soon but I'd love to talk with someone. You finish up here at the desk, clock out, do whatever and I'll meet you there in five minutes.

***

First, close your eyes, David. Relax.

You've had a long day of work. Relax. Focus on your breathing.

I'll explain later.

Focus on your breathing. In, *phhhh.* Out, *shhhh.* Listen to my voice: *Vande gurunam charanaravinde.* I bow to the Lotus feet of the Guru. *Sandarsita svatmasukhava bodhe.* The awakening happiness of the self is revealed. *Nihsreyase jangalikayamane.* Beyond better, acting like the jungle physician. *Samsara halahala mohasantyai.* Pacifying delusion, the poison of samsara. *Abahu purusakaram.* Taking a form of a man to the shoulders. *Sankhacakrasi dharinam.* Holding a conch, a discus, and a sword, for his quest. *Sahasra sirasam svetam.* One thousand heads white. *Pranamami patanjalim.* To Patanjali, I salute, *OM,* OM—that will do it, David.

Did you like that?

It's called the opening prayer.

At the beginning of class I lead my students in chanting the opening prayer of Ashtanga in Sanskrit. It helps us prepare. Lots of toxins to clear, especially in L.A. Anyway, who's ready to talk.

***

When I walked in here, right off the bat: *beep dink chink, beep dink chink*—the sound of the slots threw my energy for a loop. My head was a pinball and my body the machine about to tilt, not to mention my chakras, totally off. Somehow, I managed to spin over to the registration desk. You were there, looking swamped.

I entered the Luxor at about two this afternoon.

I know you can't forget that line. It looked thirty deep. All dudes in five-gallon hats, bedazzled blazers and knee-high boots. What about the ladies in those weird ruffled dresses of assorted colors? I wondered where the corral was. And the horses.

Yeah, I know all about it.

I asked some dude in front of me and he explained in a southern drawl that a square-dancing convention had rolled into town. He offered me comp tickets to one of the signature galas. I sighed. You'd think a yogi would be patient but I hate lines.

When I finally made it to the counter you looked funny—

Well, not funny.

You were sweating and your black beard glistened. You had all this nervous energy but you still smiled. I told you the reservation was under the Dumas party.

Dumas. Dumas. Let me see, you fiddled with the computer, ah, yes, Margarita Dumas. Checked in two days ago. I see you in here as well, Mr. Ellipses—you couldn't pronounce my name. Lipsiznowaz. It's pronounced Lips-Is-Now-Was. I had to show you a license before you issued a key for the room, the Thoth suite, on the ninth floor.

I don't have to repeat what you said. Humor me. I like imitating your raspy voice.

Excuse me?

Sure. A Shirley Temple for me. Wanna drink, David?

Any beer?

Grab him a Red Stripe. Here's twenty, sister. Just keep it.

You're welcome.

Nah. I drank enough tonight, David.

So, anyway, you can imagine how eager I felt to lock eyes with Margarita. I wanted to lose myself in her pupils, those little black bubbles. I wanted a cuddle session so I could hold her tight and long and remember why I came here in the first place.

Quit being facetious, David.

Anyway, I rushed upstairs eager to see Margarita. The room manifested niceness.

Two-fifty a night, you say.

You see. How could Margarita afford a place like that? You know she wasn't even there. I looked in the bathroom, on the patio, for some reason I looked in the closet, well, not only was she not in the room, there existed not a note, message, hint or clue of her whereabouts. I called the front desk. No messages. The fear crept in and when I worry, I turn to yoga stretches, the sun salutation, downward dog. Hang in the resting position until I relax. She'll pop up. Probably went shopping. It seemed logical enough.

I'll tell you what I did.

I hit the pool downstairs, took a sauna, a long steam, I had to sweat it out. I killed almost two hours then ventured back to the Thoth suite. Still, no sign of Margarita.

But the red message light on the phone blinked.

After consulting the phone's directions, I dialed the voicemail system and heard Margarita's high-pitched squeaky tone. It was about time. She said on the message, Keith, meet me at the King Tut's lounge in the Luxor at 6:00. Right where we are now.

Nope.

No sorry, no mention of her location, nothing like that, but she did say she'd explain it all later, and her voice appeared a little rushed. The digital red clock ticked 4:46. Time to shower, get dressed, who knows, maybe even play a little roulette, and I recall feeling a pang of hunger and thinking perhaps Margarita would want to eat hibachi.

***

Meanwhile, I dropped a quick hundred dollars at the roulette table. Fifty on red, it came out black, fifty on red, it came out black. It was the last of my spare cash, and I thought, while waiting on an ATM line seven deep, how can I live in Vegas if I gamble?

Yeah, I like to gamble a little. Something about risk.

So, despite the ATM line, I made it to King Tut's lounge by five after six. Once again, no Margarita. To make matters worse, your stupid lounge singer took the stage.

Took a seat in the back of the room, back over there, and ordered a Jack and Coke. Now, I don't drink a lot, but that guy, whew. Where do you acquire your talent?

By six-fifty the table was littered with four empty Jack and Cokes. My chin rested on my palm. The waitress tried to clear the table but I told her to leave the empties where they were. Mind you. I didn't want to sit by myself. I felt really depressed when the crooner sang "I Gotta Be Me" and for the first time I thought about going back to Los Angeles. Probably would've if you hadn't plopped down beside me with that concerned look on your face. The fax, remember? I read it to myself. Keith. Margarita's in big trouble. Go to the Hard Rock Café Casino. Lorraine. I thought who the heck is Lorraine?

You asked if everything was all right. I didn't know if I should get involved. That's when you spat all that wisdom with the force of an enlightened sprinkler. Remember what you told me? You said there are things you run away from and there are things you chase. You said sometimes different characters will have different agendas. I felt like everything was a big cosmic mistake. You told me follow your mistakes.

That's when I asked if you were a guru and you laughed.

Right. You told me you used to teach creative writing.

I'm not sure, David, but I still think you're a bodhisattva.

***

Let me get you another beer. Hey, sister. Can you grab my friend here another Red Stripe, please? *Nah, this time start me a tab.* And keep them coming when he's low. All right, where was I?

Right, the Hard Rock.

Tell me what you think of this.

I'd been wandering around the Hard Rock like a hopeless fool when I heard my name called. I turned around. Keith, a girl said again. She wore the uniform of a casino dealer. She looked pretty, dark skinned, with her black hair slicked tight in a ponytail. I never saw her before, but I will say she carried herself solid. Like a sister who knows what she wants and how to get it. She grabbed my arm and turned me around. Keep walking, she said. She let go of my arm and distanced herself slightly. She said her name was Lorraine, even though her nametag read Sarah. When I brought that up, she told me not to worry. She said she was Margarita's sister. We walked around the outer ring of the casino pit along the marble floor. I said I didn't know Margarita had a sister. You know what she said? There's a lot you don't know, Keith.

No. I wasn't suspicious. I was confused.

Lorraine said Margarita was hiding because she was in trouble. *I'm not sure, some sort of bad dealings—she wouldn't go into details.*

Lorraine wanted money so I took out what I had in my pockets, seventy-eight dollars. It happened so fast. I wanted to help. Then, out-of-nowhere, two gentlemen flanked Lorraine and grabbed her by the arm. They looked like pit bosses, dressed in suits. They both wore tinted glasses, and they both had microphones in their ears. I believe your break is over, Sarah, one said. Before I had time to react they shuffled Lorraine toward an unmarked door. As they took her away she turned around to look at me and there was a slight look of terror across her face. Without a scene she disappeared.

Exactly, what was that about?

I was thinking who were those guys? How come Margarita never mentioned she had a sister? What did Lorraine do? I walked in a complete circle, and then, the weirdest thing: winners. They were right below me, in the pit. A young couple had hit a jackpot. The coins dropped *chink bink dink*. They were newlyweds. He wore a tacky hat that said just married. A nice crowd had gathered that included two square dancers in full regalia.

***

About Margarita. She was never the type to find trouble. I dated girls that caused trouble. Girls I had to defend against other men, girls that would get drunk and create negative situations, but Margarita never did anything like that. In the two months that I knew her there was never any conflict or confrontation. I tell you. It felt like pure being!

I met her in class.

She was a good student, quiet and obedient. She never did anything wild or spontaneous. She seemed smart, precise and cute. I always felt comfortable around her. I never had to worry. And she was like a content cat when we cuddled, practically purring, her small figure clinging to me. She would tell me her dreams of being an actress. How she always had a passion for the stage, but how it was so hard. She always said, many are called, few are chosen. I had such pleasant dreams when Margarita slept over.

I don't know, stuff. We used to watch a lot of movies.

That's none of your business, brother.

I just wanted to find her. Everything was sooo weird.

Bullshit. I felt extremely worried.

You don't think so, huh? I couldn't imagine the problem. I wanted to find her and wrap my fingers in hers, like I used to do when we walked down Sunset Boulevard after seeing some play at the Tiffany Theatre in West Hollywood. She represented the only reason why I left L.A. You know that, right? I don't know Vegas. I don't know why Margarita came here or why she said she needed a change so bad.

You're right. Change may be essential in a character's life.

All I know is I liked the look in her eyes. I figured I could teach yoga here, you know, give it a whirl. I thought I loved her, but I wasn't even sure that I knew her, but in plain English she had said she loved me, and I'd travel to Antarctica for a chance at love.

You told me that she checked in here two days ago. I thought maybe she came to Vegas a week ago and must've won a ton of money, so then she checked into the Thoth suite. I figured things must have caught up to her. She must've blown the money back.

She wouldn't have lured me here for money.
She knew I didn't have any.

What money did I have? I came here with nine hundred dollars to my name. She must've somehow borrowed money and landed in a bad place. That's what I thought. But who really knows? It's easy to jump to conclusions, particularly when incommunicado.

***

So, for the second time in two hours, I hit an ATM machine.

The line looked six deep and I felt hungry, anxious and deep in thought. What was that Lorraine thing all about? Things weren't clear. The idea of fasting crossed my mind when I couldn't help overhearing these two guys behind me. How could anybody not hear them, they spoke so loud. They babbled on and on about hookers. You know the type. I bet you get a couple of questions like that a night. Well, they wouldn't shut up about the infamous Chicken Ranch. They had a menu of some sort, and one went on about wanting a half and half, or better yet, a reverse half-and-half. The other guy desired dessert. He said he wanted the Frappe French. It's when a girl goes down on you with an ice cube in her mouth. But the ranch was too far, they said. Then they went on about the different pamphlets they picked up on the strip. Lucy the college girl, Li the Asian and Saz the dominatrix, they wouldn't shut up. I'm telling you. Those two looked determined to lasso in a couple of hookers before the silky moon gave way to the rising sun.

I was like, brothers, enough with the hooker talk already. David, women are divine minstrel goddesses, they're not real estate, they're not for rent.

Anyway, I started getting antsy in that line and said so. Lot of lines in this city, one guy said. I agreed. Lot of lines. He rubbed his nose and sniffled giving me the impression the lines he referred to were white. He introduced himself as Winfield. Said him and his partner Russo were lawyers from Tacoma. I told them I was looking for a girl named Margarita. Russo gripped my hand harder than necessary and asked if I knew where they could score a cheap hooker? You could tell Russo hadn't slept in a while by the way he swayed. What do you think,

David? People don't sleep much in this city, huh?

You're right. I bet they don't meditate much.

Anyway, I was next up for cash when Winfield swore to me that they'd met a Margarita last night at the Bellagio. It had just hit him. He described her right. Short, dark skinned, brown eyes, straight black hair. Winfield said he asked her if she was a hooker, and she threw her drink at him. Then Winfield and Russo started arguing.

Russo said, no, you're wrong, stupid. We we're drinking Margarita's last night at the Bellagio. The girl who threw the drink at you was named Amber. No, you idiot, we were drinking Amber Ales, the girl was Margarita. No, the girl was Amber. Margarita.

You're right, I do like doing voices.

I do act, why else would I live in LA?

***

Outside the hotel the Vegas sun descended into the western horizon and everything within my panorama, the palms, bushes, cars, clouds, signs—everything took on a vibration that anticipated the evening. It was the magic hour and the energy pulsed in the air like Peruvian shrubbery in *The Celestine Prophecy*. You ever read that book?

You should.

So, there I stood outside the Hard Rock Hotel meditating on the magic hour when I remembered Margarita mentioning a while back that the New York New York was the coolest hotel on the strip. She said we should plan a holiday there one day. Of course, intuition tickled—an inner voice—it whispered loudly, go to the New York New York.

Now, as you know, David, a Las Vegas night is truly like no other, even I knew that, but when I first saw the lights of the strip, whoa, I bought into the dream. Power, luminous power, electric action, vibrant chaos, all so enchanting. All that glitter's is not gold. Yeah, whatever. My yogi senses went *bling* and then shut down with overload. All I could do was smile as the cab rolled down Las Vegas Boulevard.

When I walked into the New York New York the sound of the casino had a rhythm that inspired energy and confidence. Every *beep dink chink* still random, but within the boundaries of order. I mean I could sense the next *chink,* man. The rhythm of the slots like bebop—*scibbity-bop-da-bop-bop*—it made me want to gamble. Was I conscious enough to realize the gamble of chasing Margarita? No. Why I didn't realize that and stick to the task, blame it on the spell the lights cast. The city lights. They were bigger than me, man. But everything happens for a reason. I've always believed that. So what if I wanted in? I wanted to play. I wanted to play something tangible, something moving with the *beep dink chink*, not blackjack, or poker, or the stupid slots. I needed to control the risk, have it in my hands, so naturally I ventured to the craps table.

***

You know, David, I don't mean to digress, but you have to take this trip down memory lane with me, cool? The way I learned how to play craps is funny. Like in fourth grade. While the boys were busy bouncing rubber balls and scooping up jacks I was fiddling with my stones. I loved collecting crystals. Hematite, jasper, topaz, pyrite, agate, obsidian, quartz. You name a crystal I had it. I kept them in a special pouch I wore around my shoulders. What was the name of that pouch? Let me think. Oh, yeah. It was an Ethiopian book satchel. I kept the crystals in my Ethiopian book satchel. One time we went on a field trip to the Legion of Honor, way out in the Richmond District, I grew up in San Francisco, you see. The trip occurred in early autumn, fourth grade; a Book of Kells exhibit was on loan from Trinity College. From that exhibit I learned about the satchels. They were popular back-in-the-day with the monks and the missionaries who spread the good Christian word. The satchels were loosely bound, made of rough leather, perfect for carrying a script. That Halloween I was an Irish missionary. I made a cloak out of potato sacks, painted my arms red, and my eyelids black. I found a long walking stick and sanded it smooth. And I stitched my Ethiopian book satchel out of cardboard and a purple Crown Royal pouch that I had found. But instead of the bible I put Archie comics in the pouch and instead of the Christian word I wandered around the neighborhood spreading a notion I called Jugheadism. After Halloween I kept the pouch for my crystals. About sixth grade I invented a game with the crystals, played with chunks of green jade, waxy black onyx, orange amber, and pointy purple amethysts. You'd get a shoebox and toss the four stones. The idea was to keep the onyx away from the amber. You'd roll until the onyx was the closest stone to the amber. You wanted to get as many rolls as you could. This was a few years before I knew anything about their metaphysical properties. Like why would I want to attract amber to onyx in a game when they're both grounding stones and are naturally attracted anyway? What did I know then? I just loved the colors. I had this one amber rock with remains of a moth fossilized in the resin. You could see the remains of the fly. The moth was probably a million years old.

That's not true, David. I played sports.

I was really into baseball. I collected the memorabilia too. I like lived for the Giants. And this was when they sucked. Long before Barry Bonds. I could throw out names like Candy Maldonado, Joel Youngblood, Chili Davis. Those were my heroes.

But in Middle School I used to play crystal craps with some of the kids in my class. We'd even gamble on it. It was fun until Tyrod the bully got sick of losing and threw my amber crystal so far it flew out of the playground, across the street and onto the rooftop of a Victorian. Then we used dice and Tyrod taught us to play craps.

***

At the table, the guy rolling, of all people, was a square dancer.

Easy. Fifty on the Don't Pass line. First roll he crapped out. Next guy I didn't bet.

I didn't feel it, that's why.

Please don't patronize me about my New Age sensibilities, David.

Anyway, next roller was me. Fifty on the Pass, boom, seven. One hundred on the Pass, boom-boom, eleven. Two hundred on the Pass, boom-boom-boom, seven. Fuck it, four hundred on the Pass, boom, nine. Ten on each of the hard ways, fifty on the Field, boom, hard ten. One hundred on the Field, *boom-shalack-lack*, snake-eyes. Three hundred on the Field, *boom-shawalla-walla*, hard four. Six hundred on the Field, boom shebang bang, nine. Number nine. Number nine. Number nine. Like the Beatles song.

You're right, like the Thoth suite too.

Just like that, David. In less than five minutes I was up over twenty-one hundred. Just like that. Quickest five minutes ever. Five minutes of fun. Five minutes of release.

I don't sound like myself?

I did get a little excited there, huh? *Phhhh. Shhhh.* It was just five minutes of life. I walked away. Would you? Could you? I was looking for Margarita. But dig this, David.

On the cashier line a young man in a tuxedo approached me. He introduced himself as a pit boss. He had slicked back hair and a devilish grin capped his aura of fake modesty, besides, I never trust a man with an earplug, whatever he's tuned into can never be as interesting as my own thoughts when I'm in good form. And after a streak at the craps table of course I'm going to be feeling some vibes. The pit boss asked me if I was leaving. I decided to play with him. I said something like to leave implies an arrival, sir, and I'm merely passing through. Then he came back with 'we here at the New York New York,' blah, blah, blah, appreciate your custom, yadda yadda, he gave me a comp for their steakhouse. I took it, but I don't trust those types. They're very shady. Then real sarcastically I said thank you very little and shook his hand. And he said, dig this, you're quite welcome, Mr. Lipsiznowaz, you can be fortuitous for so long, and he walked away.

I didn't.

No, it didn't hit me at first.

I was at the cashier sorting chips then I jerked up. How did he know my name?

You think it's getting weird now.

***

My stomach grumbled a seven point two on the hunger scale. All I could think about was food. The comp heated up my pocket and my pallet salivated over the idea of a free steak. Now usually I'm a hummus and kelp man. When the hell do I eat steak?

Fasting was out of the question. I couldn't concentrate enough to fast.

So, there I was, on a long line outside Gallagher's Steakhouse, thinking how the hell did that pit boss know my name? Did Margarita know I'd come looking for her at the hotel and leave notice? How did they recognize me? And what was I doing in Vegas waiting on line at a steakhouse? I felt like brainless cattle and you know how I hate lines. Then I thought maybe Margarita would be eating a pastrami sandwich at one of the hotel's delis. Totally random. But I walked around the Village Eateries, through their version of Times Square, along streets complete with smoking manholes. I picked up a turkey sandwich and peeked into a variety of pizzerias, cafes, delis, and ice cream parlors, lazily sorting through a myriad of gluttonous fools like they were the baseball cards of my youth. Scrub, scrub, scrub, doubles, scrub. I shuffled through the pack hoping to find the one card I wanted: Margarita. No such luck. Not in New York. And then, happenstance, karma, I don't know what, David, but that's when I met Boom Boom.

Yeah, Boom Boom. That was his name.

Wish I never met the hustler too. That cat was a character. You tell me? Are there really people like this here? Or is it all fantasy? This guy looked like a seventies pimp.

I'll tell you.

He had on a blue velvet jumpsuit. He sported a mini-afro and rocked more jewelry than Sammy Davis. He stood on the side of the manufactured street with a sign that read 'need help.' You need help, I said, regaining the playful mood I was in after my winnings. Don't look like it with all that jewelry. You know what he said? I think you need help walking around New York all alone like you think you Kool Keith.

Oh, right away, it was the first thing out of my mouth.

He said I don't know you. Kool Keith is a rapper I dig. I didn't believe him. I asked if he worked for the hotel, if he knew Margarita. He said I work for Boom Boom. The hotel's just my place of business, and they cool with me, like I'm cool with Keith.

No, I wasn't scared.

I thought the way the night was going I was supposed to meet this guy. He was fated to help. He said his specialty was assisting people to find what they needed and he could tell I was looking for a girl. He asked if she was worth two c-notes. I dug into my wad and fingered two bills. I slipped it to him as inconspicuously as possible. He said go to the Bellagio, look for Uncle Vinny, and tell him Boom Boom sent you.

This happened, David.

I can't believe this place, but it happened, man. It happened so freaking fast too. It was like he was Huggy Bear from *Starsky and Hutch* and he knew the word on the street.

I'd usually never give some dude two hundred dollars. I had so much.

Twenty-one hundred dollars was a lot to me. And this was a few hours ago, when I still cared about finding Margarita. But as Boom Boom strutted down the fake New York streets, the 'need help' sign under his arms, I was alone, more confused than ever.

***

Clock struck nine and I decided to walk toward the Bellagio.

That's the thing, when I came here, I didn't sign up for a struggle.

Outside the New York New York it was too bright and loud: the roller coaster up above zoomed, the show at the Excalibur across the street filled the sky with fire, the MGM exploded in a soundtrack of self-promotion, and people loomed everywhere. And not only young swingers like Winfield and Russo, but families, scores of people, their eyes all reflecting the desire to surf the electric hedonism that flowed in waves along the boulevard's currents. I wasn't buying it like before, but I drank it. I jumped into the pool and headed upstream. Oh, man. The hordes of people, the rush, it felt hectic. What's the hurry, I thought, feeling overwhelmed and depressed. Was I supposed to find Margarita in all of this? I passed the Monte Carlo and the Aladdin was across the street. Where do all these people come from, dude? And how many lines are there to wait on? The taxi cab, front desk, ATM, the shows, blackjack tables, buffets, rides, the traffic, nothing but lines, nothing but lines. What American decadence created these lines? I can imagine some Goliath of a spirit devil, a soul addict, some demon that lives by ciphering spirits. I can imagine that demon spirit sniffing the long lines of Vegas to get a fix, to get the light.

It shouldn't be a part of life. Oh, David, how things go in cycles.

It's like the popularity of Vegas equates to the resurrection of sin, and then the need for redemption returns with a resurgence of religion, God is no longer dead, sin is no longer in. The lines in Vegas shrink, but never totally disappear. You feel me?

Dude, I'm sorry, I guess you do get used to it.

My mood changed too. I passed the Boardwalk and across the way Bally's and The Paris; I took it all in. At first, I brooded, sorry Margarita, I can never live in this city, but then, but then, but then I snapped to attention by the beautiful eruption of the fountains outside the Bellagio. God Bless America, land that I love, stand beside her.

A patriotic rush fueled me to almost salute the magnificence of the display. The red, white, and blue underwater illumination added to the mood. You know what I'm talking about, right? The Bellagio's fountains? You've seen them? That is the American phallus ejaculating its power showcasing for the world American sorcery. When those fountains shoot skyward, one at a time, *shew-shew-shew*, one-hundred-and-eighty degrees, then thunder up all at the same time, BOOM, man, oh, man. It's like it marks an entrance to a kingdom where if lady luck has it her way anyone could reign supreme.

***

That place, whew, that place, how can I describe that place? Want to talk about creative, David. You throw an a between the p and the l and that's what that place was.

A palace, exactly.

Right from the get-go I glided along milky white marble into an open domed atrium embellished with the choicest blossoms imaginable.

I took it all in then returned to the task at hand: finding that salty *boricua* who lured me to Las Vegas with those three words which at that point depending on my mood were either revelatory or taboo.

Then: I love you. A woman, brushing by me, she almost yelled it to the man she hurried after. Her tone sounded awash in gin. I recognized her. Try to guess who it was?

No, it wasn't Margarita.

It was one half of the big winning newlyweds from the Hard Rock. Her man wasn't wearing that goofy hat anymore. I wondered what all the yelling was about.

Then I wondered how the heck to find this Uncle Vinny character? I didn't want to start asking around, did I? The last thing I needed was exposure or some pit boss rolling up on me. If it took all night, I'd find Uncle Vinny on the down low. With a little reason, and a belief in luck, the design of the day will usually fill one's cup.

No, that's mine.

You think it sounds like a Shakespearean fortune cookie?

Well, with that winged logic I skirted the casino into the Sportsbook where Fortuna herself blessed my ears. Across the room, at the window where one places a bet, a little man in a suit turned around. Yo, Vin, he yelled, the five is a late scratch in the second part of your double, what do you want me to do? He sat about four rows back, in an armchair, it seemed almost a throne. Without saying a word, he cast up a heavy hand and motioned the little man back. That had to be Uncle Vinny. That's what I thought.

That was the problem.

I didn't know how to approach him. I sat at a bar right outside the arena, ordered a Jack and Coke, and kept my third eye on the Sportsbook. I wanted to make my move after the horse race. To infiltrate the presence of a shadow like that I figured it was best for the mood to glide in under the lighted pretense of a gambling victory. He won. After the race his little friend was at the window collecting a pile of money.

Wait a minute. You want another beer?

I'll have one with you now. I'm all excited. Two more Red Stripes. Thank you, sister-love. Yeah. So when the little guy was at the window that's when I made my move. I strolled over as casually as I could. Excuse me, I don't mean to interrupt—he didn't let me finish. Sit down kid, he said, his voice a bellowing ripple. He said I was wondering when you'd get the balls to come over here.

He did sound tough.

I was a little intimidated except his lips and nails were red. It was comical, almost surreal. He was eating red pistachio nuts. His lips looked like a bad drag queen's make up. There lay a huge pile of shells on the floor. I took the seat next to him. We faced each other. He leaned forward in his seat. He had silver hair, bushy white brows, a little white growing out of the ears, a big nose, and those red lips.

I asked, "Are you Uncle Vinny?"

He said is that what freaking Boom's Boom's calling me?

Meanwhile the little man in the suit came back and looked at me with contempt. He scratched his head. I had taken his seat. Tony, go get lost for five minutes.

The little man disappeared and Uncle Vinny returned his attention to me. I was talking with my hands—

I don't know. I talked with my hands.

I said I'm looking for a girl. It seems like she may be in trouble. You ever meet a broad that's not trouble? He cracked open a pistachio.

I said her name's Margarita Dumas.

Of course I asked him if he knew Margarita.

That's who I was looking for, right?

He said he never heard of her.

I said she came a week ago—he wouldn't let me finish. He yelled are you kidding me, kid? His attention wavered, looking at the big screens, probably wondering how many minutes to post. He spoke about Vegas eating someone up, digesting them and then regurgitating them back to Cincinnati, just like that. He snapped big red fingers.

No, I was actually comfortable with Uncle Vinny. We started talking.

I said it's like Margarita's a completely different person. And he answered no one here is who they appear to be. He issued me some education. When I said I thought Vegas was a swinging place he went off. Get the hell out of here, will ya? I've been here forty-five years. This town used to be a swinging place. It had character, its own heart. Now, forget the number, now it's an institution. He looked at me hard and went on. The banks are the shylocks, the corporations the gangsters, and they know everything. They have some grip on this operation. It's tight, the walls have ears, the ceiling eyes, and they got their pit boss agents running around like soldiers. It's all connected. You're a dot, you're girl's a dot, I'm a fucking dot. Connect the dots, kid. I sit here all day in the Sportsbook, doing what I do, and they leave me alone purely out of respect for nostalgia.

That's what I asked him.

He said he was retired from construction. I asked him if Boom Boom hustled me and he said now you're learning, kid. Then the man in the suit returned to claim his seat and Uncle Vinny cracked open a nut, picked up his racing form and told me to scram.

***

You're nobody till somebody loves you, crooned out of unseen speakers. I started to think I'd never find Margarita. Something must've happened. She met someone else and split town. I thought goddamn it if I find that girl I'll kill her, after I give her the biggest hug. I'd have hugged her so hard she would've choked right in my arms, and both of us, deflated, would've spent the rest of the night in resuscitation. But I have to admit, I felt a little blackballed. I was on the outside looking in. And I had the sense of being hustled. Someone was setting me up for a takedown. But I still had a lot of money in my pocket and there were about two thousand ways to spend it.

I had been walking around the hotel aimlessly.

There was a huge line of people shuffling out of the late performance of Cirque du Soleil. I was almost stampeded by a group of square dancers. I flew out of their way and eventually landed at a bar. I told you, David, I'm not really a drinker, but I ordered a double Jack on the rocks and gulped most of it down. The whisky hit me that time too. For the first time all-night I felt drunk. And that's when the shit really went down.

Man, you haven't heard anything yet.

It started with a sultry voice: looking for company. I looked up at this pretty tan thing with long straight black locks and full lips. Her lips moved to the rhythm of her gum chewing. She looked like all the other ladies in the place, elegant, but this one wore a velvet leopard print choker that gave her away. The leopard print, the feline, the predator, always the stripper or hooker. I mumbled I'm not looking for company, I'm looking for Margarita. Check this out. She said I don't think she's here tonight, Keith.

I jumped up from my seat at the bar.

Okay. That's it. I looked up to the ceiling. I yelled why the hell does everyone know my name? Where's Margarita? What's going on? Then the girl said calm down, cowboy, don't make a scene, you don't recognize me? I looked at her hard. She did look a little familiar. She pulled her hair back into a tight ponytail, her forehead accentuated.

You got it, David. It was Lorraine.

I told her I was worried about the way those guys swept her away. That's sweet, she said. She stroked my chest.

I asked about Margarita.

She said she spoke to Margarita and she was on the down low — so to speak.

Exactly. What does that mean? But let me finish the story.

I turned around to face the bar. Across the way a man was waving his hands in the air trying to get my attention. It was Winfield. He signaled me toward him. I excused myself from Lorraine by giving her a twenty and telling her to order us a round. I walked to Winfield. He led me around a corner. When I turned the bend there was Russo, sitting on the floor, his hands covering his face. Winfield told me to watch out for that girl. Russo mumbled something about six hundred dollars. Winfield said the girl I was talking to was a hooker named Scarlet and she had just hustled them both. He said Scarlet agreed to meet them for a fixed price, one-fifty, and then got both of them real hot and upped the price to three hundred each. He said they had no other choice. They were all fluffed. He said the whole thing lasted five minutes and when they argued this big Samoan guy rolled up and made them pay it all. Then Russo reiterated Winfield's warning about Lorraine.

Well, I was skeptical about Lorraine being Margarita's blood sister, but I didn't believe Winfield and Russo totally.

Because Russo said something like did you call Sugar to get more white and I knew they were talking about cocaine so to me their credibility was shot.

I didn't want to hear it. I turned the corner and walked back the way I came.

Lorraine sipped a cosmo. A Red Stripe waited for me. I apologized to Lorraine. But then I got distracted again. About thirty yards in front of us a commotion began to boil. A couple of people were being dragged through the casino, four of the pit boss-security guard agents on each of them. You whore, the man yelled. You drunk loser, the woman screamed. Then Lorraine was in my ear trying to get my attention. She whispered do you want to help Margarita. She needs your help. Come on, Keith. Help Margarita.

The man and the woman were closer. The agents had them in handcuffs, pushing them along as fast as possible. I knew I shouldn't have married a bitch like you, the man yelled. I followed them with my eyes and my mind registered a huge Hawaiian character standing on the side appearing to watch us. Lorraine was in my ear, she needs more money; she just needs a little more. The agents had pushed the couple by us. You lost it all, you goddamn loser, the woman screamed. Guess who that couple was?

You got it, the newlyweds. The big winners from earlier in the day.

Lorraine called my name. She said are you going to help Margarita or not?

I'll tell you what I did.

I know when the energies are trying to tell me something. Like a triple lock door, my mind, heart and wallet, I bolted them all.

That was the last chip in my bank.

***

I headed back here, to the Luxor. Journeyed up to the Thoth suite, no sign of her, no note, nothing. I called you and asked if there were any messages: no messages.

Remember what you told me?

Exactly, betrayal is a major theme in everyone's life.

It's like this, David. I'm in a jungle. I'm trudging through unexplored regions, chopping out paths, a machete in hand. You ever feel like you're in a jungle? Like you're lost, looking for something, but at the same time trying to become indigenous, so that it's all yours and it feels natural. Well, I need to be indigenous to myself. And Las Vegas isn't the only jungle, and like you said, there are things you run away from and there are things you chase. Whose path is this? Here I sit, in a Las Vegas lounge, with a bodhisattva, all checked out, less than twelve hours after my arrival. I can't believe you were still working when I came back. So much happened today. Are you hungry?

No? I am a little.

Well, listen. I want to thank you for hearing me out. I have to head out, like right here and now. The last flight out of McCarron is at twelve-thirty. I have to hurry up.

Nah, I don't even want to know if you hear from her. It's too late.

But I do want you to take this.

Come on take it.

I gave Boom Boom twice that. Take it.

You've been on my side since the start.

I know it's a crazy story.

Write about it if you want to. If you still write, that is.

Definitely a lot of characters.

I don't know if anybody'd believe it though. The way I kept running into the same people. I don't know if I believe it. Maybe I'm sleeping in Los Angeles and I'm not even here, maybe this person who has been talking to you is my double, my dreaming body.

I know, I know, I'm here. It happened.

I learned a lesson too. I just have to meditate and recapitulate.

Sometimes you learn things, then forget them, then remember them, then remember to forget them. Anyway, David, it's time.

I'm going back to Cali now.

Namaste to you as well.

THE SEA LION
San Francisco, California, 2003

On a sunny summer day in San Francisco, a father wanted his daughter to witness the sea lions at Fisherman's Wharf. The sea lions were to be the highlight of a weekend holiday—the first of its kind since the divorce and displacement of his daughter into the custody of her mother over a year before. So far, the trip was a great success, and they saved the sea lions for last, despite the daughter's pestering desire to see them earlier. Arriving at the Wharf, they stood with a crowd in a courtyard, watching the antics of a robotic hip-hop mime painted head to toe in silver. Every breath of wind carried the whisperings of French, Japanese, German, English and Spanish. The sixth and universal language of rhythm rose above the chatter as a street performer pounded on a tom-tom.

"Let's go see the sea lions now," the daughter said.

They left the horde, hand-in-hand, and turned toward Pier 39.

The father sometimes worried. He didn't worry about how he would get along with his daughter or even about what her mother would think. He fretted over memories. He wanted so much for his daughter to never forget the trip. As a consequence, they were always snapping pictures: him, the mock hippie, hugging a redwood in Muir Woods; her, the adventurous nine-year-old, hanging off the side of a cable car on the top of Powell Street; natural beauty, the Pacific Coast just north of Carmel; the crazy local, the Bushman.

Twenty years later, they could look at the photographs and the father could say, "Remember this picture? Remember the guy who hid behind the bushes and barked at us like a wild dog when we walked by? He scared us silly. Oh yes, you were very much scared. Please. Remember how fake those bushes looked? Where was that? The Wharf?"

"I hear the seals hang out on rocks."

"They're sea lions," the daughter corrected.

The father did not want his daughter to recall *a* trip to San Francisco; he wanted her to remember *the* trip to San Francisco with dad. Thus, he equated the sea lions with genies. She'd think: I saw the sea lions as a kid. I saw them with my dad.

They walked on the black asphalt stained with bird droppings. An empty pack of cigarettes littered the ground. The daughter broke free from her father's hand and deposited the litter into an old barrel. The barrel lay next to a four-sided bench island boxing in beautiful blossoms. "Take a picture of me with the flowers," the daughter said.

She sat on a bench beside the bouquet. *Snap.*

The father took a picture.

The pair continued along the courtyard. In one hand, he carried an FAO Schwarz bag filled with the day's souvenirs: a Gonzo Muppet doll, an "I Love SF" mug, a Hard Rock Cafe tank top, a box of Chinese medicine balls (with a yin-yang design), and Ghirardelli chocolates. In his other hand fit five warm fingers and the soft palm of his daughter.

Near the entrance to Pier 39, there stood a hollow bronze statue of two sea lions kissing. The display stood eight-feet-tall and 10-feet wide. "Go stand by the sea lions," he told her.

The daughter obliged. She posed—the sun in her eyes—without smiling. The slight irony of two sea lions embraced in matrimony flew over the head of the naïve father; his daughter, although not aware, indeed did not smile as the flow of human traffic paused. *Snap.* He took a picture of his child and the big hollow bronze sea lions locked in a kiss. She continued to pose until the paused tourists played on through.

Near the entrance to Pier 39, attached to the bridge that crossed Jefferson Street, there was an old wooden sign that featured a cartoon sea lion. The caption read: *Follow Salty to see the California Sea Lions.* Salty pointed toward the end of a long wooden pier.

The father and daughter began a quiet walk down the pier at arm's length from each other. To their left, the harbor docked numerous sailboats. To their right, behind old rusty doors, the restaurants, and shops of Pier 39 operated. Along the seascape, the Golden Gate Bridge glistened, a lighthouse flashed forever on lonely Alcatraz, and the inlet stirred with activity as Wave Runners, speedboats, sailboats and yachts carved trails of whitewater in the bay. Near the end of the pier, one tier of wooden bleachers was set up to view the sea lions. They stood empty except for two couples and a straggler.

"Where are the sea lions?" the daughter asked.

The father and daughter leaned over the railing and peered into the dark water. Three rows of 10 wooden floats gently rocked. The floats vacillated slightly, anchored by chains attached to tires thrown around thick wooden poles that jutted out of the water. Pigeons and seagulls lined the floats. The birds stood in the abstract graffiti of their dung.

"This must be the wrong place," the daughter said.

"No. This looks like the place. See?"

A few feet away lay a weatherworn sign, off-color due to the salts of the sea. It hung against the banister of the pier. The father and daughter read the sign to themselves:

THE SEA LIONS HAVE MIGRATED SOUTH TO BREED AT THE CHANNEL ISLANDS. THE CALIFORNIA MARINE MAMMAL CENTER SPECULATES THE SEA LIONS ARE LIKELY TO RETURN THIS FALL.

The father and daughter stepped back from the railing and sat beside each other on the bleachers. Far away, boat-horns blared. The breeze howled. A flag rattled. A gull gawked. A squeaky door opened at Pier 39's mall and bells from distant cable-cars rung.

"Stupid freaking seals," the daughter said. She began to pace.

The Apostasy—a boat taking tourists to Alcatraz—left Pier 41 in a trail of spray.

"Do you want to go to Alcatraz, pumpkin?" the father asked.

The daughter continued to pace back and forth. "This stinks."

The father stretched out his hands for his daughter to come to him. "Come on, pumpkin. Let's go to Alcatraz instead."

The daughter walked past him, then turned around. "Who wants to visit an abandoned prison?" She wandered to the end of the pier and stared out toward Alcatraz.

The father sat with his hands over his face. With both hands, he slicked back his oily hair. He sighed, walked to the railing, and watched the floats swaying in the harbor.

In-between two rows of floats, a single sea lion popped its head out of the water. Its long whiskers glistened in the sun; the sea lion looked around and then submerged.

"Pumpkin," the father yelled. "I see one!"

The daughter turned around. She wasn't into it. "What?"

"A sea lion." He pointed to the water.

"Where?" She looked at the empty wooden floats.

"I just saw one," the father said. "In the water."

"Whatever." She turned back around.

"It was just here." The father stared at the dark water.

In the gallery, the couples paid no attention.

A straggler observed the scene like a game of tennis.

The father glanced to the end of the pier where his daughter stood, her back to him, staring at Alcatraz. What a vision to see, his daughter set against an abandoned prison—his daughter living within the shambled realm of his failed marriage; her helplessness while stuck in the prison of a cracked family. This irony he felt acutely.

"My princess," the father whispered.

She wants a sea lion. I can give her a sea lion. The father gently put down the shopping bag filled with the day's souvenirs. He threw the camera from around his neck into the bag and began to quickly undress. He took off his shoes, socks, shirt, and slacks.

The young lovers, straggler, and another recently arrived family stared at him.

The father climbed to the top of the railing and balanced himself.

"Baby—look at me. Look at dad!"

The daughter turned around in time to see him flip upside down into the air.

She ran to the spot where he leapt. The father laughed as his head spun. The daughter, along with the onlookers, watched the water. The father's glistening head emerged, and he looked around.

"What are you doing?!" the daughter yelled. He swam toward the floats. "Get out of the water!" she said. "You're going to get us in trouble."

The father plopped onto a board. The birds dispersed. Arms to his side, he flipped and flopped around the float.

"*GNUNGK, GNUNGK, GNUNGK,*" he squealed.

"You're crazy, daddy!"

"*GNUNGK, GNUNGK.*" The gallery laughed and went for their cameras. "*GNUNGK.*"

The solitary sea lion stuck its head above the water again.

The daughter grabbed the camera from the bag.

Snap. She caught the picture.

CHEZ WHITEY'S
Dumbo, New York City, 1996

Marcus stood at the end of Washington Street egging Kinetic on with a bottle of Cisco. Kinetic swayed outside the café, the white doors his only barrier. The summer sun, high in the sky, caused the silver door handles to sparkle. Kinetic tugged open the doors and walked inside. The place was library quiet—just a few whispers from the scattered customers in for a late lunch. The walls were white and the floors white marble. So much white for a restaurant, yet to Kinetic it seemed dark in there, especially for lunchtime.

The host-stand hovered in front of him like a tollbooth.

"It's dark in here," he said.

The hostess snickered. He could feel her eyes.

"I'm hungry." He inched closer.

"I'm sorry," the hostess said.

"I get money, money I got," he lied.

The hostess grinned at his singing. "We have a dress code."

She pointed at a small sign that read 'proper dress required.'

Kinetic's hair a nest of nappy little black curls jutting out of a blue New York Mets cap; his wife-beater endured a tomato sauce stain from a calzone eaten two days ago; his jeans crumbled at the hips and rips around his knees, thighs and ass seemed to wheeze, the denim fibers clinging for dear life. Kinetic wore no socks in his old black Fila sneakers. His little pinkie toe, calloused and awful, stuck out of the right shoe.

He examined the reservation book.

"You ain't busy." He smelled drunk.

The hostess looked upset; her space violated. "You're going to have to leave—"

"Ain't no trouble—"

"—before we call the police."

"—don't be *skared*." He looked her in the eye, holding the glance until she turned away. "I'll be back. You'll see." The hostess shook her head, as if she really cared.

Kinetic walked outside. He ambled over to Marcus and handed him five dollars.

"Told you they ain't servin you," Marcus said, passing the Cisco.

"It ain't as simple as black and white." He refused the drink. "Double or nothing."

"Aiight," Marcus said, "bet."

***

People called him Kinetic. People in the park where he nodded out at night, the park in the Dumbo district of Brooklyn by the two big bridges connecting Manhattan and Brooklyn. Kinetic loved the bridges. It was all about the bridges by the park in the Dumbo district of Brooklyn where people called him Kinetic. His given name was Leroy Davis. Why did people call him Kinetic? He had energy—the dude liked to sing—in fact he often felt powerful, especially when near the bridges. To him the bridges represented New York. And New York represented America. And America ruled the world. So, if Kinetic had the bridges, then whose world was this? Maybe it could be his world, if he had the bridges. Sometimes it felt like he had the bridges when he stayed in the park in Dumbo because the bridges were there. And it felt like they belonged to him.

That is, before *Chez Blanco's* opened its big white doors across the street. *Chez Blanco's* with its white brick storefront, with its white awnings, even the pigeon poop appeared camouflaged at *Chez Blanco's*. Stupid *Chez Blanco's*. With its glitzy crowds, its employees in white jackets, valet parking glitzy cars. Opening those white doors for glitzy women. All summer long, Kinetic dreamily split his glances between the looming bridges and the glitzy people outside of *Chez Blanco's*. What did they have that he didn't? For one, they had *Chez Blanco's*. So maybe it wasn't his world, or even his city; maybe the bridges didn't belong to him. But they could. Or could they?

***

Kinetic borrowed a radio from Marcus's cousin's girlfriend's brother Maurice.

He stood circled by a group of tourists in front of a Midtown deli off of 8th Avenue. The radio played an instrumental tape laced with heavy drumbeats over slow bass chords. A tip box sat on the ground in front of the radio. Against the wall, lay a forty-ounce of Old English and a pack of Newports. Fully animated, hands gyrating to the rhythm of his tongue, Kinetic did his thing. *"It's the Goosebumps you get when your friends succeed / it's like getting high for the first time off of weed / it's your nose in her hair taking in that aroma / your boy in the crash just came out of the coma / it's that feeling you get when the Knicks whip the Heat / it's a kid on Halloween yelling trick or treat / it's a feeling in life, a feeling that's free / I feel so fine, I hope you feel me."* Two young Japanese girls wore bright garb radiating an electric rainbow. One dropped five dollars into the tip cup. Kinetic bowed. The Japanese girls curtsied and walked away.

After the crowd dispersed, Kinetic grabbed the tips, shut the radio, reached for the 40oz, and sat against the wall. Sunlight shined on him as he counted the twelve dollars and fifty cents, he earned rapping for the past hour. Then a dark shadow blocked his light.

"You again." The officer stroked a black billy club. "Didn't you learn your lesson?" His shiny badge read Harrison. "If I see your face again, I'm taking you in." Harrison towered over Kinetic. He raised his voice. "And dump that beer before I write you another open container ticket you can't afford to pay. You must like jail, huh cutie?"

Kinetic rose and stood face to face with the cop. He looked Harrison in the eye. He turned over the beer and the beer trickled down the dirty sidewalk to the dirtier street.

Kinetic grabbed the radio, tip-box and cigarettes. He strutted towards Grand Central Station, his head up, and he rhymed for three more hours in the tunnels connecting the subway lines. Nothing was going to stop this man. Not even nothing.

He rapped until he had sixty-eight dollars.

***

Kinetic skipped down Jay Street toward Brooklyn Bridge Park. His smile looked like the quarter moon above, like Mac Tonight. Still, no one recognized him along the cardboard skids of the park. He saw the familiar faces, downcast, sullen, hungry and tired; yet no one recognized him. His main man Marcus didn't even recognize him.

"Yo, Mark-ass," Kinetic rapped. *"Don't be a pawn, I spawn kingdoms with my rook, read you like a book, no crook, but I took you for a ride, made you look inside—"*

"What happened to you?" Marcus jumped up.

Kinetic had cut his hair. Cut close and clean on top, it faded progressively shorter down the sides. He donned a white collared shirt by Ralph Lauren. The pressed shirt tucked into a pair of khakis, with a black belt around the waist. Kinetic wore a maroon tie. Maroon suspenders. He also donned light brown socks and brown loafers.

"Recognize. Thirty bones at the Goodwill."

"You look tight, son. But the glasses are too much."

Kinetic wore a pair of round, small framed, non-prescription glasses.

"Going incognito," Kinetic said.

"For real? What's the dills?"

"Whose world is this?" Kinetic sang, looking toward *Chez Blanco's.*

***

This time he walked right up to the host stand.

"Welcome," the same hostess said. "Do you have a reservation?"

"Whatever's available."

"Party of one?" the hostess asked. Kinetic nodded. She looked at the reservation book. She flipped the page. Then she flipped it back. The young hostess looked at the seating chart and then turned around and scanned the restaurant. She turned back and looked Kinetic over. "Right this way, sir." Kinetic sat in a booth against the far wall.

The waiter approached. "Expecting someone?"

"It's justice, man." Kinetic looked up seriously. "Just us."

"Us?" the waiter asked.

"Me, myself and I."

"Would you like a glass of wine, sir?" The waiter held an open bottle. "Tonight's house wine is a California Sangiovese." Kinetic held out his glass as the waiter poured a sampling. He washed the wine around in his mouth and swallowed. The waiter hung on.

"Worst shit I ever tasted," Kinetic said.

"We have an excel—"

"Hennessey, in a chilled snifter." He waved the waiter away.

The bus boy, a young Spanish man, brought water. Kinetic slid him two bucks, then looked around the room—about three-quarters full—and nodded. *Figures I'm the only brother eating here.* But he was no different than anyone else. He belonged there just as much. Kinetic felt perfectly all right until he opened up the menu. Cous cous-what, fried cala-huh, grilled porto-what, stuffed arti-who, aspara-what with holland-huh, what liver, tenderloin bro-where. What the fuck they servin here? The waiter returned.

"You have ribs?" Kinetic asked.

"We don't serve ribs, sir. However, our Seafood Brioche special is fabulous."

"I don't want no special seafood. I'm hungry."

The manager walked by and overheard. "Is there a problem?"

"It's all-good," Kinetic said.

"Seafood is our specialty. Fresh from South Street. Have you tried it before?"

"This is my first time here."

"You come to Chez Blanco's, you must try the seafood. Please, Chad. Set him up with the number three special. And bring him another drink, on the house. Make him feel at home. You sir, enjoy your meal. I know you will. And if you need anything, just ask."

"Aiight." Kinetic nodded. He loosened up and looked around the room, trying to catch eyes. No one noticed him. After one more drink Kinetic felt dizzy. His thoughts lost in the shadows of the white marble, the silhouettes of waiters carrying trays, and one elegant lady on the way to the restroom. The shadows had a patterned life of their own. Kinetic felt lethargic and didn't know why. But he also felt hungry. Soon the food came.

The Seafood Brioche special consisted of lobster, crab and shrimp, swimming in a creamy white asparagus sauce, overflowing in a bread bowl. "Things are changing." *I eat shrimp and lobster*. Kinetic dug in. *Good life for me cause I'm no imposter*. He ripped off a piece of the bread bowl. *Good Times like JJ Walker*. He spooned up big chunks of the seafood. *Strictly butters for the real New Yorkers*.

White sauce drooled down his chin.

Kinetic nodded as he went for the white napkin that rested on his lap. It was then that his throat, lips and tongue swelled up. Kinetic dropped his fork. The utensil clanked against the plate. It came fast: the hives, nausea and increased heart rate. An intense feeling of dread filled Kinetic. *I knew they were pushin the seafood for a reason*.

Everyone in the restaurant noticed Kinetic heave like a wild beast. They all heard the *thump, thump, thump*, as he banged on the table, like an insecure or tyrannical judge trying to get order in the court. And everyone in Chez Blanco's heard the crash when Kinetic flailed his hands and knocked the snifter, plate and water off the table. The waiter and manager ran over. Kinetic's hands went to his throat. Everyone noticed poor Kinetic, all eyes on him, as he rolled back in the booth, and then fell on the table unconscious.

***

Kinetic dreamt he walked atop the Manhattan Bridge. He lost his footing and fell. When he opened his eyes, he lay in a white hospital room with a white bearded doctor named Fox, and his main man Marcus. "You've had an allergic reaction to a certain fish," Dr. Fox said. "You went into a mild anaphylactic shock. We had to pump your stomach."

"Food poisoning," Kinetic said, a little raspy.

"You need to stay the night," Dr. Fox said. "There's a chance for a relapse a few hours after the incident. We want to keep an eye out, but you'll be fine here, Mr. Davis."

The doctor left the room.

"Got you candy," Marcus said, handing over an Oh Henry. "If you hungry, later."

"I'm aiight," Kinetic whispered.

Marcus told Kinetic how there was a big scene outside of *Chez Blanco's*. An ambulance and three squad cars rolled up. The paramedics raced inside with a stretcher. How he watched from the park as they rolled a black man into the ambulance. How he asked the manager what happened. He told the manager Kinetic was homeless and saved money to eat at the restaurant. The manager felt impressed and agreed to cover the hospital bill. He offered Kinetic a job handing out flyers for a club associated with the restaurant. That is, if it felt all right. The job paid fifteen dollars an hour, off the books.

"Promote Chez Whitey's? I won't play that."

"Well, at least they served you. I guess we even now."

Marcus walked to the window, opened the blinds and stared out at the lit city.

"Fuck Chez Whitey's," Kinetic said. "And fuck Brooklyn, Marcus. I'm going back to Long Island City. *When you're playing four Queens, you don't fold.*" Kinetic propped himself up on the pillows. He only had a little strength. "Marcus." Kinetic turned toward the window. "Do me a favor, homie. Shut them blinds. It's too bright out there."

PACE
New York City, 2002

On a Delta flight heading into LaGuardia, I was reading the November 4th, 2002, issue of *The New Yorker*, cover to cover, and at the theater section *ba-boom bam boom* fireworks exploded: Al Pacino on Broadway. Actually, not quite Broadway, but the National Actors Studio at Pace University. And it wasn't just Al Pacino, but Al Pacino, Tony Randall, Chazz Palminteri, John Goodman, Charles Durning, Steve Buscemi, and Billy Crudup, all in one production of "The Resistible Rise of Arturo UI." *The New Yorker* summarized it as a 1941 Chicago-gangster parable about Hitler's ascent to power. I said Al Pacino's on Broadway and that's my main man. I felt excited but fidgety in the little window seat. I couldn't take it. Everything a compartment. Me a compartment. My gear in an overhead compartment. My books stored below, compartmentalized. And the lighting, oh, the lighting, a tired dim dipped in fluorescence. And those plane people. Those cranky, tired, red-eyed plane people. Those sleeping, escaping, reuniting, business flying plane people. Those farting plane people. I couldn't wait to land and breathe the autumn air of New York. On the plane the air went *shhhhs* out of the little plastic nipples next to the reading lights *shhhhs* something like the suction catheter a dentist puts in your mouth to suck saliva dry *shhhhs* a reminder life was a vacuum trying to cipher my time *shhhhs* it wouldn't stop *shhhhs* it didn't stop once the whole time. Then the seatbelt sign illuminated. Man, oh man. Al Pacino is on Broadway.

***

As soon as we taxied an operator at Telecharge informed me of the schedule for "The Resistible Rise of Arturo UI." The price of tickets stood at one hundred dollars, but there was one problem. All the remaining shows were sold out. Three scheduled performances remained: Friday and Saturday night at eight o'clock, and a final Sunday afternoon matinee at three-thirty. No tickets left, was that supposed to intimidate me?

Here stood the logistics. I arrived early Friday and departed late Sunday night. I had family commitments Friday and Saturday night, and I wanted to hit two museums. I only had a hundred dollars cash and a credit card with a hundred and fifty left on it.

From LaGuardia I took a ten-dollar shuttle bus that dropped me off across from Grand Central on Park Avenue and 42nd Street. The plan was to stay with an old friend of my father's named Jerry Dome. I never met the man. He lived on 38th between Lexington and Third. My father told me that Jerry owed him his life, so of course I'd be welcome there, but just watch out because Jerry was a little nuts. The sixty-year-old Jerry spent fifteen years of his life in Sing Sing. On top of that he was a neat freak. If Jerry were too much, I'd stay with my brother in Brooklyn, even though he had roommates in a studio.

The doorman buzzed me up to the seventeenth floor.

I gently knocked on 1712 and a little man with golden hair, a silly grin and a face that looked like it had some work done, opened the door and gave me a warm welcome.

"You're Johnny Fats' kid. Come in."

The place looked impeccable. Not a thing out of order. You could've eaten off the floor. The living room had its couch, carpets, two chairs and coffee table. In the dining room, there was an oak table with four oak chairs. The windows, with the curtains opened, had a nice view of 38th Street heading up the Westside. The television showcased the OTB channel, where the first race at Aqueduct had thirty-two minutes to post. "Sit down." I sat on the couch, but as soon as my ass hit the cushion: "Not there," Jerry screamed, "that's where I sit. You sit on the chair." So, I bounced to the chair, no qualms.

"Let me tell you something, Jimmy—"

"I'm Junior. Jimbo's my brother."

"Come on, Junior. Let me show you your room."

I followed him down the hall.

"Don't touch the walls," he screamed. "And don't go in the kitchen. You need anything, just ask me and it's yours." He led me to the guestroom. The room looked huge and clean. There was a king size bed, marble floors, a private bathroom, mirrored closets, and the same amazing view as the other room. "Whatever you say, Jerry."

"Here." He rummaged through the closets throwing sports jackets on the bed. He grabbed a long gray ankle length Irish tweed coat. "Try this on." I looked at myself in the mirror. "It's yours, Junior. That coat's an Irving Baron. That's a thousand-dollar coat right there. Here," he said, picking up a brown sports jacket off the bed. He looked at the lining. "This jacket is from Barneys. It must have cost at least four hundred dollars."

"Where'd you get it?"

"Don't worry about it."

It was one of them literary jackets, with patches on the elbows.

"It fits nice, Jerry."

"It's yours."

My old man must've really done something for this guy.

Jerry left the room as I tried on coats. He came back with a bag of sunglasses: two Modos, two Guccis, and a pair of Hugo Bosses. "Split these with your brother, Junior."

"Are these real, Jerry?"

"Get the fuck out of here." He handed me a key. "I need to fill my OTB account. Come and go as you want. You'll be on the doorman's list. Just don't touch the walls."

"You and your walls." I patted him on the back.

***

Walking in Central Park, I entered at 90th street by the Guggenheim and stuck to the trail east of the reservoir. Within seconds, leaves fell. One leaf, rocking down, *swish*, with grace, *swoosh*, yellow, a hint of red, *swish*, it would soon be brown and crumble. Another leaf surfed the current down, one last hurrah. It landed as far away from the branch that bore it as the wind allowed. Another leaf, right before my eyes, spiraled straight down, a green silhouette against the sky. It landed two paces ahead of me on the soft dirt. After a little walk, I sat down on a hill off the reservoir near the East Meadow.

All the trees looked like V's or Y's over big barks of O's, maple and oak O's, the branches triangular V's, jutting Y's. There's nothing like Central Park in November. I took in the constant sound *shhhhs* from the traffic *shhhs* not horns or sirens but the sound of pure motion *shhhhs* the sound of tires moving in a circle *shhhhs* the sound of life.

It's impossible to be alone in the park with only the squirrels and the falling leaves. Central Park is not like Golden Gate. There one can get lost in the redwood grove by the Rose Garden or find sanctuary off the beaten path of the waterfall at Stowe Lake. In Central Park, the dog walkers and joggers are perpetual. In three days, not one New Yorker smiled at me. Try to go one day in San Francisco without a smile. Everyone should live in New York as long as they get the fuck out before they're hardened, just as everyone should live in San Francisco as long as they float somewhere else before they're too soft. I lived in old slow Miami. I only hoped I left before I died. Pace is everything.

Three cops galloped by, the hooves of the horses digging into the soft path. A mother quickly followed, pushing a twin carriage with two children. Their fast pace reminded me of "The Deluge" scene in Bill Viola's "Going Forth by Day" installation at the Guggenheim, before the flood, before the cleansing, during the panic. In 2002, you were no longer allowed to sit down and chill in New York—a cop on horseback asked me for identification. I explained I was a graduate student up from Miami for the weekend, that I'd hit the Fifth Avenue museums and wanted to walk in the park before nightfall.

"Am I suspect? Do I look like trouble?"

"It's not that, sir. But you can't sit here. You have to move."

You need people like me so you can point your fingers and say that's the bad guy.

"I can't sit in the park?" I felt angry.

"Just the times," the cop said. He handed me my Florida Driver's license and advised me to head toward the street. *Say goodbye to the bad guy.* Somewhere across town, Al Pacino sat in a dressing room getting into character for his second to last performance of "The Resistible Rise of Arturo UI." *There's a bad guy coming through.*

***

I felt like shit. I leaned up in bed and rubbed my hands through my hair. It was 12:30, Sunday afternoon, and extra warm in Jerry's guestroom. Somehow, I made it to the kitchen to help myself to some coffee. Jerry sat in the living room, on his chair, talking on the phone. "Hold on, John," he said. "Hey, Junior, get out of there." He barged into the small kitchen. "What do you want? Coffee? I'll get it, you fucking alcoholic."

I showered and drank coffee while dressing. My wallet housed a putrid twenty-three dollars. I also maxed out my credit card out the night before at 7B, a bar in the Bowery. The play started in three hours. In the living room, the OTB horse channel advertised one minute to post for the second race at Aqueduct. "Jerry, who do you need?"

If he won the race, I was going to ask for a loan to see the play.

"I got the four and the six. I'm alive in the Double."

"You didn't use the three?" The three was the 8-5 favorite.

"Who taught you to handicap? Your father? He knows nothing."

The four had the lead running the first half-mile in forty-five and one. "Quick half-mile, Jerry. Fast pace. The four may have nothing left."

"What do you know about horses?"

"Are they on the inner track?" The ponies run on the inner track during the cold months. The surface is harder and less apt to freeze, fast horses often last wire-to-wire.

"Not yet, Junior."

As the horses approached the far turn, the four put the six away.

"You're looking good."

The four, at eight-to-one odds, had a three-length lead going into the final furlong. We watched the three fly by him in the final fifty yards to win by half a length. The favorite closed like gangbusters, coming out of left field.

***

Wouldn't ask Jerry for a loan. My brother didn't have any money. The clock ticked 2:05 when I hit the streets, rocking the Modos and Irish tweed coat. It was a nice fifty degrees. I walked up Third Avenue, spending $8.59 in a deli on a pastrami and Swiss on Rye. My pockets were down to fourteen and change when I spotted the OTB. Two dollars on the program, two for the subway, it left me with ten dollars to parlay.

The fifth at Calder was an allowance race on the turf for non-winners of three other than maiden, claiming, or starter. I saw something I liked. A gray horse named Monkey Wrench. The horse hadn't been out in five months. Classy colt. In his last race he closed well to finish fourth in a Grade III at Belmont. Trained by Mott, Coa aboard, the horse had a lot going for him. Monkey Wrench, the five horse, was three-to-one. I spent the next few minutes trying to hook up the second horse for the exacta. I made two five-dollar exactas: five over the one and six. Long story short, Monkey Wrench won going away. The six finished second. The exacta paid $27.40. My voucher read $68.50. With a hundred dollars I felt I could've found an extra ticket so I bet two more races, the fourth at Aqueduct, and the first at the Fairgrounds in New Orleans.

I lost thirty dollars.

The time ticked ten minutes to three. The play started soon.

***

I made it outside the National Actors Studio at Pace by a quarter after three. The first thing I did was head inside to the box office. Maybe there was a rush ticket, a cancellation. Sorry, nope, no way, not today, nada, not even nothing, good luck, kid. The crowd around me started to bubble, a lot of scurrying. I hung like a hanger by the coat check next to the will call, hoping to relieve someone of their extra ticket. I heard one man ask an usher if the actors mingled after the show. At 3:20, I walked outside, almost feeling defeated. I stuck a finger in the air. One finger meant I needed one ticket.

"I need a miracle." I paced with my finger in the air.

"How much do you have?" the man asked.

He was with a woman.

"I only have forty."

"The ticket cost one hundred."

"I can mail you the difference if you want. Please, sir."

"How do I know you'll mail me the difference?"

All I have in this world is my balls and my word.

"Give it to him, honey. The show's going to start."

"Well—"

"I'll give you face value." A man's voice came from behind me.

"You have a hundred dollars?"

"Right here." The man gave up the cash.

"Sorry, kid."

The three of them went inside the theater in a New York minute. I don't know what to say really. We're in hell right now. We can stay here and get the shit kicked out of us, or we can fight our way back into the light, we can climb out of hell, one inch at a time. It was 3:25. I held my finger in the air. "I need a miracle." Now I can't do it for you, I'm too old. When you get old in life things get taken from you, that's a part of life, but you only learn that when you start losing stuff. You find out life's this game of inches, the margin for error is so small, one half a step too late, one half a second too slow, you don't quite make it. I had that ticket. I had it. The inches we need are everywhere around us, kid. You fight for that inch. The scene dwindled, everyone was already inside. I thought about sneaking in the back. Maybe a side door, or a ladder to the roof. I could try to bribe the ticket collector. You claw with your fingernails for that inch because you know when you add up all those inches it's going to make the difference between winning and losing, between living and dying. I had to try something.

I walked around the back of the theater. No door, no ladder, nothing. And then, bada bing, about halfway down the street, there he stood, black leather trench coat, big broad shoulders, tall like a skyscraper, all by himself in a cove, smoking a cigarette: Chazz Palminteri. Guy's probably trying to get into character. It didn't matter. I walked up, looked up, and can't even quote what came out it happened so fast. I talked with my hands, just the thumb, index, and pinky. Up from Miami, grad school writer, theater lover, parlayed last ten bucks at OTB, almost had a ticket, blasé blah, trying to sneak in.

"I like your sunglasses," he said, in a slow tone.

"My sunglasses?"

"I just lost mine."

"Here, try em on. If you want, keep em. They look good on you."

"You got a phone?" I handed him the cell. He dialed a number. "What's your name, kid?" I told him my name was Junior. "Are these Modos?" He mumbled my name into the phone, took a pull off the smoke and flicked it. "Go to Will Call. There's a ticket for you." He turned, with the glasses on, and entered the alcove door.

Fuck the Modos, I thought, my shades are yellow and red, the shades of a northern leaf in November. Then I walked to the front, clicking my heels like a kid who just kissed a girl for the first time.

THE GREEN CRUSADER
San Francisco, California, 2003

I left prison only two days ago. I stayed incarcerated ten days, two hours and forty-five minutes. Spent eight hours in County Jail Number Nine, near the Hall of Justice on Seventh Street. That was for booking. They took a mug shot, fingerprints and my freedom. Then a night in County Jail Number One for further processing: psychological profiling, medical inquiries, things like that. Finally, I spent nine grueling days in County Jail Number Five: it's a special ward at the General Hospital. I had no calls, no visitors. Some hero, huh? They kept me in my own room too. You know: a room with cushioned white walls. This is San Francisco, dude. Trust me. I'm not that crazy.

Can you imagine a small room with a fluorescent light hanging from the ceiling, lit for sixteen hours a day, buzzing? There are people who deserve to be locked up—murderers, rapists, pedophiles, some Republicans—but what did I do? Who did I hurt?

At least they didn't keep me in population with those animals, with the real criminals. They would've eaten me alive. Me, a skinny white brah with long bleached blond hair. They would've said, little surfer boy, come here little surfer boy. Who am I kidding? I wouldn't have survived ten minutes in population. I'm so stupid. Can you believe I laughed? When they arrested me at the museum. I laughed. After ten days in county jail, I'm not laughing anymore. What bothers me is that he left me in there. Greg could've bailed me out. He's the crazy one. Leaving his only son in jail. They should put him in there for neglect. You know what it is? Greg thinks I want to embarrass him. Stain his good name. All of this isn't about him. It's not about Greg. I stumbled onto something big. He should stand by my side. Oh, no, to him, I'm just tainting the good old family name. And don't get me wrong, dude, to some extent—I totally see his point-of-view.

***

It took him ten days, but Greg came through.

He posted my bond.

I gave back the county orange uniform. They issued me my stuff: my faded denims, white tee, wallet, cigarettes and baby blue lighter. Describing my stuff, I sound like some greaser from the Fifties. Like some Fonzie wannabee. Or like Schneider from *One Day at a Time*. Yo, Mrs. Romano. I'm here to fix your pipes. Whatever. Those jeans are my favorite. I remember when I first ripped them. I was with Sky, rock climbing, up in Mendocino County. There's nothing like getting your stuff back. It's your stuff, man.

Greg waited for me outside in the green Lexus, the car running. I saw the frames of his glasses staring at me. You'd think he'd step out of the car to give his son a hug. No. I had to knock on the window for him to unlock the door. It was freezing in the car.

"Do you need the air on so high?"

He looked at me with those squinty eyes. The look told me he took this thing more seriously than I did. And it's not that I think this thing is a joke. They don't have a case. I mean really. Throwing money into a toilet and shitting on it, come on, bro.

"This isn't like the time they arrested you for writing graffiti," he said. "Desecrating American currency is a felony. Did you know that? You're in trouble."

"It's like burning the flag. What happened to freedom of speech?"

I asked the wrong question. He banged the steering wheel. His slicked back locks bounced out-of-place. "You didn't burn the goddamn money. You fucking shat on it."

We started moving. I tried to make my window go down.

"Greg, can you unlock my window, please?"

It felt like forty degrees in there. Who uses air conditioning on a sixty-five-degree day in San Francisco? And I totally hate when he does that window locking power trip thing, man. Like he's a window Nazi or something. Finally, he unlocked the window. As I watched the glass fall, the breeze naturally warmed me up. Let me tell you a little secret about myself. I absolutely relish the wind. I love the way it feels when it slaps me in the face. It's like skydiving. It sets me free. And I love the sound of the wind. Like an empty tunnel, lonely yet personal, it sings to me. That sound. It's like a void. It's like being inside a tube on my surfboard. Time stops. I feel safely at home. And I like it.

"Your story was in all the papers and on the local news," he said.

I figured as much. There had been a feature written about me in the *SF Weekly*. They painted me favorably, like a local weird Robin Hood. In fact, the *Weekly* coined me the Green Crusader. Turns out the attention backfired. The cops mentioned it when they arrested me. They said the article encouraged them to hunt me down. They said an idiot like me who throws money away doesn't deserve his freedom. A couple of rookies on the force took it as a challenge. Greg rolled my window back up and locked it.

I looked at him and smiled.

"I'm a minor threat. It was my money."

"It was your grandfather's money, Gregory."

He raised his voice.

I know what you're thinking. You think I just wanted attention. I told all of this to Greg. I'm not denying it, at least at first maybe that had something to do with it. That and boredom. But I definitely stumbled onto something. If you saw those faces holding a shit stained hundred-dollar bill then you'd know what I mean. It says something about our society. It does. That's why I did it. And that's why I continued to do it. Maybe I wanted to get caught and that's what the card was for. I'm not sure. I started leaving a little calling card at the scene. Just a white business card with the initials GC printed in bold. But the GC doesn't stand for the green crusader. It stands for me, Greg Canting, you know Canting, of the Canting property developers. Name's got clout in California. But so what? And what's wrong with being recognized as some Robin Hood? I made the discovery. It was my mission. What's wrong with wanting some attention? You tell me.

"How much money did you waste doing this?"

"I stopped counting."

"The news reports estimate fifteen thousand."

"I started so long ago."

"Twenty thousand?"

"More like thirty."

I'm glad he had both hands on the wheel because I could sense his losing control. He rolled down the windows for some fresh air. "You're a sick individual, Gregory."

***

When I first started, I used to hang around to see the results. I'd linger, like a foul odor, outside whatever joint I cased. And I traveled all over the city, believe me bro.

I hit restaurants like "A Connecticut Yankee" in Potrero Hill, "Godzilla Sushi" on Fillmore, "Crepes on Cole" in Cole Valley. I hit public bathrooms in Golden Gate Park, the Kabuki theatre, that famous bookstore in North Beach. I tagged nightclubs like the Boom Boom Room, Slim's, the EndUp, Café DuNard, the Top. I hit johns in Pac Bell Park, 3Com Park. I flagged nursing homes, car dealerships, coffee shops, massage parlors, grocery stores. I hit every district except the Presidio because that's where I live; but Nob Hill, Richmond, Castro, the Marina, Chinatown, the inner Sunset, the outer Sunset, the Mission, Russian Hill, the Wharf, you name it; even Berkeley, Oakland, Sausalito, Mountain View, San Jose, the whole damn Bay Area. I was out of control.

I had a routine. It's a little gross. I would eat as much cheese as possible. I used to eat a lot of burritos and omelets and pizza. Or just beans out of the can, mixed with handfuls of shredded cheese. I would always try to eat some asparagus too. Then, before I was going to hit a place, I'd down the largest iced coffee I could get my hands on. Within minutes, my stomach would grumble. And then: show time. I'd hit the stall, drop the hundred-dollar bill in and let the deluge out. And it came out, dude. Not in chunks, but in a fast spray. The diarrheic shit would stick to the bill getting inside the fibers of the paper. Then, I'd squeeze out a little urine, just to make the place smell extra bad. I would wipe, but I wouldn't throw the tissue in the toilet. I left it on the floor.

After the first thirty times it didn't matter, it became useless to linger. The results, of course, too predictable.

People grabbed the money. Every. Single. Fucking. Time.

***

The bottom line is I'm not greedy. There exist mad greedy people out there. People who want more than they need. I don't have responsibilities. I don't have children. I'm a young punk, sure. So what if I threw thirty g down the toilet and another twenty-five lost bailing me out of jail and some more on lawyers. We're worth millions.

I would've bailed myself out, but I don't get my fund for another two years, when I turn twenty-one, unless I get Greg to authorize some purchase. But I do get a thousand dollar a week allowance. Over the course of a year, it wasn't hard dropping thirty grand.

Let me put it this way. I have money so it's a little easier for me, but what do you really need in life? Not much. If you'd ask me that question, I'd answer good eye contact and a pure smile, not money. Whatever with business. The rat race is just not natural, nor organic at all. What's the point? It seems like a catalyst for self-destruction, right? These capitalists. They feed on growth and their appetites are insatiable. They all want a piece of the pie. No more pie? Then what? They still feel hungry. So it's onto another pie and another. What happens when the Earth closes its kitchen? I couldn't explain this to Greg. He could never understand. I don't need or want money. I could sustain myself on the bare essentials. As of late, I've only been interested in trying to co-exist with Sky. And also, my diet. This crusade took a crazy toll on my body, nutritionally. I'm particularly looking to cut down on dairy. Or maybe go completely raw; except I'm hungry, like a lot.

***

This whole thing started as a joke, a stupid little experiment. A test of human nature if you will. I wanted to see what man would do for a hundred dollars. And I learned something. Who would've thought how low a man can sink? Would you dig through shit for a hundred dollars? I know I wouldn't. And neither would Sky.

On occasion Sky would come with me. I liked that. She'd hit the lady's room. I'd hit the boys. We'd never wait. I knew the results. Someone was sure to walk in and a couple of minutes later, there they stood, shit eating grin. Their shirtsleeves always stained and wet. We'd laugh as we continued on to the next one. It's disgusting, really.

You know who inspired me to do this shit, right? Of all the brothers I know, Murphy. That dude probably wouldn't remember if I asked him, but that's Murph for you. He's that kind of burnout. When around him, if you're real quiet, you can hear his brain cells sizzling. But I remember. At the beach house in Santa Cruz on a Saturday afternoon. Sky, Murph, me and the overcast day. The ocean looked too choppy to surf. Murphy tried to go out anyway, the crazy cat. He didn't care. I stayed in my room with Sky. We lounged around. Puffed some nuggets. Watched *Fast Times at Ridgemont High*. A half hour later Murphy wandered back into the room, still wet, his dreads shaking water all over the place like a dog just given a bath. "Too choppy," he said.

Sky and me smiled. Murphy eyed the leather futon next to the bed. He threw some clothes on the cluttered floor. My long board blocked his vision so he moved it to a corner of the room. Sky packed a bowl of this Haze from Humboldt she had. I passed Murphy the pipe first. It's proper etiquette, except he smoked all the green. But we still got high. We just chilled watching the movie and like fifteen minutes later I smelled something burning, like dry wood, or paper, like a campsite late at night. I looked over at Murphy and there he sat, mesmerized, holding a dollar bill lit on fire. The bill was right in front of his face, and he waved it in the air so it burned faster. I nudged Sky so she could check him out. Just when he was about to burn his fingers, he extinguished it in an ashtray. "Murphy, what are you doing?" Sky said.

"What?" he said. "It's only money."

***

Last night my father invited me out to dinner. Actually, he insisted that I go. He wanted to talk about things. But he did say I could bring Sky along. He had us meet him at this nice place South of Market. We had to get dressed up fancy. The place looked cool. The walls painted an ox blood red, with the floor tiles the same color. The tablecloths were silky black. Combine that with the candles that burned on every table, and it made it feel like dining in hell. Totally cool vibe. Except, from the very start my father seemed bent on making us feel uncomfortable. "They want you in a medical facility up in Vacaville," Greg said, before we even opened the menu. "We can beat this, but it won't be cheap. You have my name. You may not care about this, but I do."

"I don't want to talk about it," I said. I felt like I said everything I needed to say in the car after he bailed me out. Anyway, I truly feel like they don't have a case.

We tried not to talk about it, successfully for a while. We talked about sports, history, his childhood, his father, celebrity stories, basically a bunch of sentimental shit. Sky talked about the city's problem with the homeless and life in Arcadia, where she grew up. We also talked a lot about my mother. Greg told me stories of their courtship, anecdotes about my baby days, days long gone, days I couldn't possibly remember. We spoke about things we all did together. She died when I was eleven so of course I remember a lot. We reminisced about the trips we took together. We were always traveling. That trip down memory lane brought him to the exact place I tried to avoid. "You know, Gregory, your mom would be so disappointed in you right now."

***

My mother represented a real lady. She loved me. I would've been out in a few hours if she were alive. For sure she would've stood by my side. I'll give you one example of mom's love. That time at the big game. When I was ten Greg pushed me into Peewee football. Even then I quietly believed football was a game for barbarians. I was learning how to skate. I wanted Greg to help me build a quarter-pipe or a rail-slide. He made me play football. The big game came and like the last play they threw the ball to me. I caught it and ran toward the end zone. They chased. I ran. I felt absolutely no glory in running, and then boom, I got popped. I coughed up the pigskin, some other kid picked it up and ran it back for a touchdown, we lost, and of course it was my fault. You could feel the vibes from my teammates, their parents, the coaches. Everyone thought it was my fault. That's what made me cry. I didn't even want to play. They blindsided me. Who stood there to hug me and wipe my red eyes with a soft hanky? Who gave me love? Not Greg. He was in Long Beach on business. He could never make the games, but she always came through. My mother always came through.

***

Sky excused herself to go to the bathroom. She stood up and disappeared into the shadows of the restaurant. Because of the candles, that restaurant had the coolest shadows. Greg didn't pause for a breath. "Your statement? It's against me, isn't it?"

"Against what you stand for."

"And what's that?"

"Taking material things and trying to build them into something real," I said.

His nature is not that of a giver, it's more like a buyer, just like his father. Business first—buy, build, buy, build more, building—it's his business. He doesn't know any other way. He sees building as something he can buy. But his eyes don't represent my eyes. I can see for myself. "I want you out of my house," he said. "Tomorrow."

We sat silent for a few moments until Sky returned.

My dad smirked. "Now, excuse me," he said. "Hopefully, there's no surprise for me in the bathroom. If I had a pair of gloves, I'd dig through shit for a hundred dollars."

"I bet you would," I said.

As Sky sat down, my father stood up.

He walked off toward the restroom.

***

I thought Sky was the coolest sister in the world. I really did. First, she's so smart. She always read. Sky turned me on to Tom Robbins. She'd read all his books. A smart sister is so important, you know, and Sky, well, she also involved herself in things too; she was always going to rallies and protests and signing petitions and what not. She motivated me in that way. Like at the Free Tibet Rally, a big group of us, about a thousand deep, we all marched up Market Street chanting 'Shame on China' and 'Free the Panchen Lama Now.' We wound up outside City Hall at the Civic Center and there stood another protest, this one about gentrification in the Mission District. We jumped protests because Sky's that kind of person. And Sky is a lot of fun too. She isn't super serious or anything. We always did fun things. Like snowboarding in Tahoe during the winter, or surfing in Santa Cruz, hiking in Marin, picking strawberries in Watsonville, whatever the case. And Sky looked so cute. She was a total hottie. She always wore these hippie dresses and you could see her whole bronze back and there rested this little tattoo of Ganesha on her shoulder. It drove me crazy. She looked so cute. And she acted like a freak too. We used to do it at least twice a day. And in the weirdest places. We did it in elevators, in the ocean, the woods, on the airplane to Maui for that weekend last April. But the best was when we'd chill in my room and the candles and sage burned and she'd whip out those silky red fetters and tie me up and come at me like Medusa in the dim light, her dreads alive, she'd lick me all over and I surrendered, man, I was hers. I think with Sky I never figured out the difference between lust and love. That's a hard one.

***

I didn't waste a minute.
"Babe, how long we with each other?"
"More than a year already."
"Maybe it's time we get a place together."
"But you've been in jail. You might have to go back."

"Ten days, Sky. I've been gone for ten days."

"A lot can happen in ten days."

"What are you saying?" She said something. I could tell by her body language. Her eyes wouldn't meet mine. She seemed jittery. "Don't hide anything. Stay in the truth, Sky. Isn't that what you always say to me? Who is it? Tell me who it is, Sky."

"Murphy."

"That wanna be Rasta. He's an impostafari."

"And you're a trustafari, Greg."

Sky paused. She picked up a fork and pointed it at me.

"Nobody's authentic. Not anymore."

"You could support me. I need you now."

"Greg," she said. "Every time you gave me money, I never did it. I kept it all."

I had her all wrong. Her free spirit didn't come free after all.

My father came back. I stood up.

They asked me where I was going.

"I'm not as hungry as I thought I was."

I threw my napkin down and walked away, into the shadows. I stopped a waiter to ask the whereabouts of the bathroom. He pointed to the left of the front door. In that area was a plush maroon waiting couch, a fireplace and the restrooms. A family of four waited on the sofa. There sat a kid. He must've been about twelve. He rested on the edge of the couch, his back to his family. He didn't want to be there, you could tell he'd rather hang with friends, probably skating. He had a biker chain wallet and dangled it through the air letting it fall on the floor. I used to have a biker chain wallet just like that kid.

The fireplace stood between the ladies' and men's room. A soft fire flickered. It warmed me instantly and for a moment I lost myself in the flames. I looked at the gentlemen sign attached to the oxblood door. The kid's chain made me think of jail. I didn't want to go back. Meanwhile, Sky and Greg walked toward me out of the shadows of the restaurant. I bolted outside and marched in the direction of the nearest corner. A homeless man lay camped near the curb passed out cold. I paused. In my sports jacket I had a wad along with one of my green crusader cards. I folded a hundred-dollar bill into quarters and placed it, along with the card, in his calloused hands. Greg and Sky yelled my name. I turned a corner, crossed the street and flagged down an oncoming cab.

DOLLY & DIAMOND
San Francisco, California, 2003

Dolly:

Didn't have a pen. Who could afford a pen? I used a cork. Diamond was proud of my genius. Way I burned the end of the cork. I burned the bugger till it looked all nice and chalky. I adjusted the cardboard and scribbled **L O N G S T O**. Then I burned the cork again **R Y A N Y T H I**. One more spark was all I needed **N G H E L P S**!

Diamond:

The story of Dolly and me? I'll spill it. We lived under a bridge at the intersection of highway 101 and Cesar Chavez for about a year. There was a core group of us about fifteen deep. That's where I met Dolly. I loved the bird right from the start. She was so flighty she needed a safe place to land. And the bridge seemed straight. Kind of like a family. We even stayed cool with the cops on the beat. They knew we were harmless. We were down with Caltrans, too. Caltrans made a deal with us. They said if we kept the area clean we could stay, could even keep our carts. They helped us. They dropped off garbage bags on Wednesday and picked them up on Thursday. We kept the place snowy clean. Nicknamed the spot El Dorado. Then around election time the mayor's office tried to come off like they found a way to co-exist with the homeless. They publicized El Dorado and shit. Made them look like they were managing the homeless problem. You can guess what happened. El Dorado flooded with homeless from all over the city. Looked like a Grateful Dead parking lot, but the family vibe disappeared. El Dorado became cliquey. Dopehead hippies over here. Crackhead hookers over there. Drunk Mexicans this way. Crippled veterans that way. Caltrans still dropped off bags, but no one filled them up. We lived in shit up to our ankles. Then the rainy season came in December and the city whipped out their brooms. The cops turned on us. DMP collected our carts. They put up a fence. They put up a fucking fence, under the bridge. If you ask me the mayor's office knew what would happen by publicizing El Dorado, but you can't fight City Hall. Dolly and me, we stuck together. We moved to Van Ness and California.

Dolly:

I love San Francisco.

Sunday mornings I leave my stuff with Diamond and take the 49 down Van Ness to Market then transfer on the 71 up through the Haight. I get off at Stanyon and walk through the tunnel into the Park. I stroll around the bend past the field where the Mexicans play soccer. Then, under the hanging foliage that's vibrant and magical like an enchanted forest, I enter the meadow. Some call it Golden Gate Park. Some call it Hippie Hill. I call it my Meadow of Sanctity. It's the little area of the park beside the tennis courts. It's especially nice when the sun hangs high in the sky. I kick off my shoes and relish the piney blades of the crew cut lawn. Then I plop down on the hill and the continual motion in the meadow is like a merry-go-round. Footballs, baseballs, Frisbees, soccer balls, hacky sacks, young girls with hula-hoops and devil sticks. Kids stream paper through the air like in a Chinese celebration. Dogs run around in packs. The meadow is scattered with folk; tribes of comrades, desperados like me. Then, at the only bench in the meadow, there's always a drum circle. The rhythm of the drum is my beacon. It's eternal.

There's always somewhere in the world where a drum's being played. Right now, in Africa, Australia, Brazil, China, India, somewhere someone is beating a drum. Bet on it. They're pounding away. Right now. Can you hear it? It's happening right now.

Drumming takes me to Orgasmo. One way ticket. That's right. Orgasmo, my Orgasmo, how can I explain you? You're beyond anything sexual, for sure. You're everything and nothing, Orgasmo. You're a void, but you ain't empty of energy. No, sir. There's energy. It's sex without sex, and there's rhythmic drumming, pounding, and a high pitch, like a dog whistle. I feel it more than I hear it, Orgasmo, and it freezes me, numbs me cold and I cling to it, and there's laughter, always laughter. And it's *all empty*, but it ain't. Orgasmo, it's the closest I can get to oblivion. Diamond could never understand you. I know Diamond can't understand. You're mine. And words can only begin to touch your surface. But on Sunday afternoons, as I lay on the hill in the meadow, under the sun, I stay with you for as long as possible, clinging to the drumming, until I get distracted. Then I pick up the Frisbee or football and toss it in the direction it came.

Diamond:

When I looked in the bathroom mirror at the McDonald's on Van Ness and Golden Gate, I swore by the end of the week we'd be off the streets. And I meant it this time. Enough's enough. For Christ's sake, Dolly's in her second trimester. It's no way to live, especially when you're having a baby. In the bathroom, I splashed water on my face. I rubbed calloused hands down stubbed cheeks. I looked droopy. I put a wet finger on my reflection and ran it down the middle of my forehead. The noisy smear startled even me. I laughed. Well, not quite a laugh, but my lips moved in an upward direction. I took it.

Dolly:

And the women in San Francisco are like fluttering sprites. Their wings are made of sugar, sweet-sweet sugar. Every filament of that wing candy coated in a honeycomb dream. And if you look in a San Francisco woman's eyes, you can see them bubble, and every time they blink a lash flirts out sparkling dust. Some swish in the air, mystically disoriented, others swoosh around in excitement. The women toss about, no judgments, in this citywide garden, San Francisco. Y'all can even catch one in your hands if you're lucky. Maybe at a park like Washington Square or outside the Funky Door Yoga parlor. Now you can catch em — but you can't keep em. They're not the fireflies of your youth, boy. You can't put em in a cleaned-out Prego jar under a lid you used a rusty scissor to puncture air holes with. And you can never clip their wings. You can only admire their beauty. Then you got to let them free to flap and flop where they will. If you're lucky they'll linger, like me to Diamond, like a moth to light, for a moment or an eternity.

Diamond:

A bus makes a sound as it roars by, an extended city-growl, intimidating and disruptive. Sometimes it spins me like a top, round and round, out-of-control, off-course, *where am I, what happened?* But only for a couple of seconds, unless, unless . . . unless I embrace the grumbling bus and let it charge me, take her in like a breath, invigorating and necessary, like *rrrrrraaahh*. Sometimes I hardly even notice the bus roar as I walk along the berry lined sidewalk faster than usual, my head held high. Maybe I crack my neck or knuckles, maybe I pound my chest. Sometimes I march on, like what, like the noise is nothing, like I belong here, like I own this motherfucking place, and I say to myself, *Diamond, you're a warrior, son, you're a warrior, chief, you are a warrior.*

Dolly:

But it ain't all sunshine, honey.

I'm tired. I mean I am *tired*. I worked the corner, sign in hand, for nine hours. It's a good corner to work too, Mission and Van Ness. I felt lucky to work it. I made more than my usual spot on Van Ness and California. Still, what did I earn? Twenty-two dollars and forty cents plus half of a club sandwich. It's not like that time in the Mission when Diamond woke up with a hundred-dollar bill in his hand. But it could've been worse, I guess. Some girl kicked down a couple of books. A college

chick with pink hair and a lip ring. She said she'd seen me reading
before and thought I'd appreciate the authors. She said they'd help me
remember I was a woman. I'm not exactly sure what she meant, but I
took the books, and, oh, speaking of kicks, the baby kicked for the first
time. I couldn't wait to tell Diamond. But as far as the books, I've read
Rebecca Wells, and Grace Paley. I never checked out Charlotte Perkins,
that's all. I love to read, always have, but out here it's different. I really
like to read when it rains. I take the blue tarp out of the cart, cover the
wagon, slip the white rope though the tarp's rings and fasten it around
something stable, like a parking meter or a sign. I give myself a dry
sanctuary under the canopy, and I read through the rhythms and the
patterns of the splitter splatter rain.

Diamond:

This cat Hector I knew from the old days when I squatted in the
Mission had it. I didn't want anything to do with it. I really didn't. I ran
into him out-of-the-blue. He said he had it and it was Peruvian and pure.
He said he'd front it to me for fifty. *One gram, ese, you can step on it.* I
stopped by the Walgreens on 16th and Mission and picked up a small
bottle of vitamin B12. It's an old street trick, vitamin B12, it has no flavor,
it's smooth, perfect color, perfect for stepping, perfect for work, some
people use baby laxative so don't give me no hard time. I got six half-
grams from one gram. This was a far cry from one of them late night
Monday recycling quests where I stumbled through the steep streets of
Potrero Hill, drunk on beer, digging through blue bins for a nickel. Those
cans and glass get heavy when you don't have a cart. Still, sometimes it's
worth the thirty dollars the Chavez recycling center gives you. And it's
kind of legal, at least harmless. It didn't take me long to get Hector's
money. In less than two hours I sold all six bags in the Mission at thirty a
pop. I didn't do any. You think I might've, huh. It was about the money,
that's all. So, I beeped Hector and met up with him at his crib. I gave him
his fifty and asked for two more grams. I paid cash and got them both
for ninety.

Soon I had twelve half-grams and forty bucks in my pocket. It was only ten past two. I hopped on the 14 out of the Mission, jumped off at ninth and bounced around SOMA making my way to the Loin. I only dealt with kids, and tourists, but the kids, the fucking college kids. That's who I looked for. Kids who walk around like addicts pushing along allowance drips. Way-y-y more of them than you think, especially in this town. Little art students from the Midwest, *here, buy some drugs*. And the tourists too. A white boy in the Loin that's not a bum is either looking for drugs or he's a tourist. Tourists keep the homeless alive. And God Bless them, too. God Bless those good old boys from the South that still have a conscience. And God Bless those European motherfuckers. And God Bless the summertime when they everywhere. If you have to hustle, and you want to stay out of jail and make some money, kids and tourists, that's the ticket—but who wants to deal with that monkey hustle shit—but sometimes to get by. Anyway by five I was out.

Three hundred and ninety-five dollars. It could get us off the streets, but for how long? I had to secure a job and a place to stay. Cause I can stay sober and get a job. No. I have to secure a job and a place for us to stay. Okay. Cause I *will* stay sober and get a job.

Dolly:

Yesterday I felt so old I thought I might die.

Y'all know the feeling?

Something in the air—more than the fog, more than the breeze— made it unbearably cold for a while. There was nothing in the air. Y'all know the nothing, right? Some electric *nada* sizzles fluorescence. The nothing, it drones overhead like a bulb. Some drowning nothing—it gripped a hold of my ankles. It tried to take me down. It sunk into my bones and made me feel old. I asked Diamond about it, and he said maybe it was my diet. Too many liquids, he said, but not enough milk. Not enough protein or calcium, or Vitamin D, or whatever it is that makes your bones strong. I saw it as some unwelcome spirit. I felt like a cavity waiting for a filling. Diamond thinks I'm far out. That ain't it.

I feel things differently, that's all.

Maybe it *was* the weather, uninviting, overcast, and dreary. Whatever the case, my house felt haunted. Maybe it was nothing.

Part Two
Little Ado About nothing

nothing **in San Francisco**
circa **2002**

Hired by Zoetrope, PG&E, Barry Zito and The Asqew Grill
nothing stole the San Francisco sun and replaced it with a cape of fog.

nothing strikes again.

Coffee sales at Rockin Java skyrocketed. As well as SF fleeces sold at the pier. And Cala
Foods had a sale on Sierra Nevada, $9.99 a twelve pack, for those with a Cala Club card.

Mayor Willie Brown, with the help of Silicon Valley technology, uncovered the conspiracy.

Exposed by *The Chronicle, The Guardian, The Street Sheet,* and *Poor News Network*
nothing needed a clean well-lighted place to hide.

i'm on the lamb.

Three places nothing hid:

1. between the cream cheese and salmon of a Philly roll at Godzilla sushi in Pacific Heights.
2. inside the gold tooth cap of a retail clerk at Mr. Bling Bling's on Geary Street.
3. within the fist of Rodin's *The Thinker* outside the Legion of Honor.

The city was a war field.
So much hate. What a mission!

Hungry as can be—nothing devoured the Tenderloin.

Jeez, i'm not Castro, thought nothing. *You win.*

nothing gave back the sun...

nothing **in the U.K.**
circa 1996

nothing was seedless and certified as
being organically grown.

One World Cup
nothing landed in Manchester, England
and picked daisies while
looking for the mothership connection.

nothing was a Guatemalan bookbag
a stitched tapestry of
dreadies, punks, Rasta's, rude boys
—a collage of masks,
a horny peacock
chirping 'one love, one love.'

History right before nothing's eyes
at 4:20 the IRA bombed the city
with carrots, cheesecake and crackers.
Uh-O Spaghetti-O

nothing thought *no one really knows if they're dreaming*.

In England the lights are red then yellow
before turning green—
there was panic on the streets of London.

In the Kyoto Garden of Holland Park
dodo birds cried of a mislead faith—
the usual non-traditional hoopla.

nothing wrote in a journal:

ideas can be solid
but they can also be waste
and it is through digestion
that one can tell the difference.

and for 1 quid 50 pence
nothing caught a ride out of Manchester
to check out the crop circles in Hampshire.

nothing **in Paris**
circa 1996

nothing was caught by MTV cameras
stealing the vandalized bust of Jim Morrison.

nothing ran to the metro, jumped off at Porte Dauphine
cut through the Bois de Boulogne and cowered along the Western bank of the Seine.

Where do i go from here?

nothing in sunglasses and a beret drank a fifth of absinth then watched *Johnny Dangerously*
at the Gaumont Italie before eating a croissant on the way to the Louvre.

There is a lot of nudity in art.

nothing needed a drink of logic and decided that the bottle of Merlot was half full.
The impeccable nothing with an unbending intent ventured back to the Pere Lachaise.

nothing noticed Officer Poncherello marching up and down the Rue de Menilmontant.
nothing entered the cemetery through the Rue de Rondeaux.

Language is the fourth dimension

nothing, Chopin, a group of non-violent German punks, Marcel Proust, an authentic gypsy,
Oscar Wilde, De La Soul, and two hundred naked freaks sat in a circle singing

breek on drue to dee otta zide.

nothing **at the 30ᵗʰ Anniversary of the New Orleans Jazz + Heritage Festival (New Orleans, 1999)**

Disguised as James Joyce
nothing played a thought-tormented
funky bass—a musical
one-hundred-fold touchdown
that caused Widespread Panic
amongst white space.
High on crystal methods

bagpipes and tom-toms
nothing smacked phrases into arms with quills:
character is destiny,
drama over explanation,
every thought leads to love and death.
nothing learned it's better to be watched than to watch,

better to pass boldly into that other world in
the full glory of some passion,
than fade and wither dismally with age.

nothing danced and danced and danced
with Truffula trees and Billie Holiday—
drank Buddhist OM's

mixed with Jamaican rum,
got drunk on frankincense,
ate cannibal kebobs smothered in hummus.

nothing vowed to stay in New Orleans
till the batteries of time corroded—
instead, exile in a Rolls Royce with
the morning dew and pieces of jigsaw.

nothing broke down in Bonifay, Florida, cried,
hitched to the Café Risque near Gainesville;
nothing bore it all,
received a copy of Finnegan's Wake—a lifetime supply,
then walked back to Brazil.

Part Three
Florida stories

THE BOX
Coral Springs, Florida, 1999

My name is Giovanni Perduto.

I work at Gino's Pizza, doing delivery.

I drive around this freaking suburb, listening to the radio, delivering food. No one bothers me. While waiting for deliveries sometimes I read. Sometimes I dream about Maria. Other times I hang in the back of the restaurant and make boxes. All in all, I work for a few hours during the day, a few hours during the night, and then I go home.

My boss Sal, he's some gambler, Sal is. Him and me, we're like family. So are the rest of the workers. Everyone's fine, except old Joey, he's a little weird. And it's not that I don't love Joey. After all, he hails from Pistoia, little town north of Florence, same town in Italy my parents come from. And he did help Maria and me. I just don't know about that guy. He had this secret you see. *Madonna mia,* did he have a secret.

I found out about a week ago.

Let me tell you something. Joey's secret changed my life.

Two drivers working, the old man and me, no deliveries. I'm in the back of the restaurant, eating a slice of Sicilian, thinking about Maria's hazel eyes. Normally I wait in the car and read, but it was pouring rain outside. One of them summer storms. They don't last long. You could hear the rain slapping the cement in the back alley.

I like the crazy roaring sound of the storm.

When I walked to the front of the restaurant and seen Joey sitting at a table reading *Time,* I asked him what was going on in the world. He told me Mel Torme died last week. I said who the hell is Mel Torme? He said the Velvet Fog. The velvet fog?

You see what I mean about Joey being weird?

Sal talked on the phone. I wondered if he was taking a delivery order, a pickup order, or if he was calling his bookie to bet on the Cubs game. I nodded in Sal's direction.

"A delivery for you?" I said to Joey.

"Maybe." He turned back to the magazine.

Joey's about seventy years old. He was skinny. He wore khaki shorts and his bony legs barely seemed attached to his tiny knees. Joey's face appeared downcast, the skin melting off like lava. And his old decrepit ears were disproportionately larger than his head. I thought he had cancer, yet that salt and pepper hair of his still shined.

"Joey, I thought when you retire, you're supposed to relax?"

"Gotta keep busy, kid."

"You just want to get out of the house, huh? Get away from the old lady?"

"Something like that."

I tore the edges off the place mat, a paper map of Italy. I ripped Sicily right out of the Mediterranean.

"Joey, you got Sicilian blood in you?"

Sal hung up the phone. "Y-o-o-o. I got a hot one. Joey, you're gonna need your box."

I've worked at Gino's for two years and there's this thing. Old Joey and his stupid box. He's got his name written in black marker on all four sides. And the box is so big. I've never seen it filled. It used to hold a case of Styrofoam cups. The old man ripped off the four cardboard lids that closed it. And with a knife he carved two rectangular handles on the side. What a Macadamia nut, this guy. He even duct-taped the handles around the top so it would be sturdy. The box looked a little dilapidated, weather worn, but tell that to old Joey and you might get slapped. Like four months ago, I had a big delivery and took his box. Big whoop. He wasn't at work when I left, but when I came back, he was outside waiting, his arms crossed like some tough guy. He called me every curse word in the book. And ever since that day he started to bring the box home with him at night. Forget about it. It's ridiculous. He looks funny carrying it. The box is as big as him.

"Joey, what's with you and that big ass box, anyway?"

"You get attached to things, kid."

"You get attached to girls, not freaking boxes."

"Yeah, yeah, how's your girl? What's her name, Maria?"

"Why do you bring the box home with you?"

"*Non rompermi il cazzo,* all right, kid."

That means don't break my balls. My pop says it too. Joey rose up and walked away. His breeze blew the shredded paper off the table. The *Time* magazine stayed open to the milestone section. A picture of Mel Torme, next to his obituary, stared me down.

***

Maria came over my apartment that evening.

I've lived on my own about three months. I moved out of my parent's house so Maria and me could get used to living together. She's always over. When I lived with my parents, they're old-fashioned, Maria wasn't allowed to spend the night. What a crime!

That night I rented a movie, and we watched it in my room, my girl and me, cuddling. Her straight black hair smelled like coconuts. I like holding Maria in my arms. It makes me feel important. I stroke her arm, making little circles, her guinea skin even darker than mine. That night I kissed her neck, gave her goose bumps, but she told me to just watch the movie. Oh, that neck of hers, I could've eaten it. We watched a comedy, but who remembers the name. After the movie, I gave her a full body massage. She relaxed and I worked those knots in her back. Maria works in a restaurant too, as a server. One of those big corporate chains. I could never work in one of them. We talked about our day. I told her about old Joey and that stupid box of his. She didn't care a lick.

"You know what's in two weeks?" she said. Maria stretched and rolled over on her back, so she looked me in the eyes.

"Of course." I nodded. "You think I'd forget?"

"Can you believe it's been three years?"

I believed it all right. It's the only thing I really believed in. Shit. Joey's not the only one with a secret. I already had a ring picked out and almost enough money to buy it. My big secret plan was to propose to my princess on our three-year anniversary.

***

The next day after lunch-shift is when I blew it. I can admit it now. I made a mistake. No doubt about it. I couldn't stop thinking about Joey and his stupid box. Why did he bring it home? It didn't make no sense to me. We both had night shift off. The box was cool at Gino's. He had absolutely no need to bring the stupid box home. Why couldn't I mind my own business? Can you believe what I did? Let me tell you what I did. I followed him home from work yo, like a freaking sick-o stalker, unseen, but there. And I must admit, even though it felt wrong, it was fun. I followed him west on Wiles Road. The setting sun blinded me. It made me put my hands up to block the light. I could barely see. But I seen Joey turn into a strip of duplex homes. I passed his entrance, made a U-turn, circled around, and parked in a complex next to his. I could see Joey clearly from my post. After he finished putting a silver sun visor on the dashboard, he walked around the side of the car, grabbed his box and took it out. He brought the box inside. I didn't expect him to. I guess I always figured he'd leave it in the car. When I witnessed that I got real curious. I read a book until after sunset. The darkness of night would allow me to feel safe. I like to read more than one book at a time. Lately, I've been reading Buddhist books. I read other philosophies, but most of the other crap confuses me. When it finally turned dark, I walked around the back of Joey's complex. What a mission!

In the backyard, there was a canal with a steep grassy bank. There's a lot of canals around here, some of them lead to Everglades, others just man-made dividers in some suburban City Planner's wet dream. Weird shit swims in these canals. Definitely some bass and bluegill but wouldn't be weird if you saw a gator or a python. I don't fuck with gators or pythons or them canals at all normally. Anyway, I crept along the canal like a rat, counting the units to Joey's place. *One, two, three, bingo.* The screen was unlocked. I walked into his patio and approached the door. It was one of them sliding glass doors.

The darkness afforded me safety. On the other side of the sliding glass window, through half-shut drapes, I could see inside. There was beamed light. It came from the kitchen. And it shined from the bulbs attached to the ceiling fan over the dining room table. I watched the fans move and for a moment I felt lost in circles, like when I played with

Maria's arms. I noticed the kitchen and dining room floors were tiled. White marble. They ended at the beige carpet of the living room. On top of the kitchen top lay a mixture of spices, bills, bananas and a knife set. His fridge had a calendar held up by Gino's magnets. That old box of his sat in the corner by the front door, right next to the stairs.

The television was on. But there wasn't no picture. There wasn't even no static. Just a blue screen, like when a DVD movie ends. Joey sat on a black leather couch, his back to me, head down. I thought he was reading. Then he stood up. He had something in his hand, long, thin, rectangular, but not a book. He had a picture frame in his hand.

Joey walked toward the kitchen and shut off the lights. He turned the fan off. The fan lights too. I don't think he saw me although he totally looked my way. Nothing to see in the dark, I figured. Then he walked back to the living room and placed the picture upright on top of the television. I thought he was calling it a night. I'll never know why he didn't shut off the television. The room appeared dark except for that droning blue light. The blue screen made me wonder about old Joey. Maybe he's afraid of the dark.

Then I really wondered about Joey when he walked over to that freaking box, put one foot inside of it, then the other, and sat down so only the top of his salt and pepper hair could be seen. I shook my head and just stared at that box with Joey in it. I almost knocked on the sliding door. The blue room. Joey sitting inside of that old box. What the fuck? I almost shook. And I heard my heart beating inside of my chest. That's when I stumbled back through the screen door onto the grass. It made more noise than necessary. I didn't care. I'd seen enough. Forget about it. I ran through the shadows back to my car.

***

The next day at Gino's I arrived before Joey. Usually, it's busy with rain in the forecast, but business appeared slow. I had one delivery in two hours. Went to the hospital. Got a three-dollar tip. Back at Gino's I seen Joey's car in the alley. It was about a quarter to five. I parked next to his car when the sky thundered and it began to rain.

Them summer storms sure can rage, but inside it was peaceful. Sal read the paper. He was in a bad mood since the Knicks lost the night before. When I came in earlier, he'd mentioned he dropped a g-note on the game and not to talk to him. I didn't want to talk to Sal. I wanted to talk to the old man. All night I thought of Joey in that freaking box. I hardly even slept. I'd been looking forward to confronting him all day.

It started to pour outside. I mean really come down. You could hear the roaring sound of the storm I like so much. Joey sat at a table all by himself. I slowly walked over.

"Hey, Gio. Some storm. Think it'll pass?"

"We'll make money."

"What's money?"

"Joey, who's in the picture?"

"What?"

It thundered and the rain continued to pour. "Last night, I saw you looking at a picture. You were looking at a picture and then crawled inside that stupid box of yours."

His face colored. He closed his eyes until they were little slits.

"Is that why you bring the box home?"

"You-son-of-a-bitch," he yelled. Old Joey showed some quickness. He jumped up and charged me like a bull. A thunderbolt crackled in the stormy summer sky. Joey grabbed my shirt and pushed me into the wall. Sal's autographed picture of Frank Sinatra fell. I heard the glass frame shatter. "You cock-sucking son-of-a-bitch," he yelled. Joey slapped me in the face with his open right hand. Clap! Like lightning. He slapped me again with the backside of his hand. Clap! It felt just like lightning. Joey slapped me again and again, each slap like a bolt. The veins popped out of his head. I was stunned. The beating didn't stop until Sal came over and hugged him off of me.

"O-o-h, calm down," Sal said.

"Who's in the picture?"

"What do you know?" Joey yelled.

"Calm down. It's all right. Giovanni, what's going on here?"

"Who's in the picture?" I fell against the wall, confused. My face stung, but it was all right. No big whoop. I can handle that kind of pain. "Who's in the freaking picture?"

Joey broke free from Sal. "My wife, all right, my wife. She died four months ago." He lowered his voice. "I've kept it to myself." Joey looked out the window while me and Sal stood still. He came back to himself. "All right? Are you happy, you son-of-a-bitch? You better stay away from my house, or, so help me God, kid, I'll kill you dead."

Old Joey headed out the backdoor right into the storm.

He got in his car and drove away.

***

"What the fuck was that about?"

"That old man is crazy, Sal."

"What'd you do to his house?"

I started to fill Sal in on the details from the day before, but I kept getting interrupted by the phone ringing. Orders kept coming in. Sal kept taking them down. In the meantime, I cleaned up Joey's mess and made some pizza boxes. I also kept wandering over to the backdoor to listen to the rain falling from the twilight sky. By the time I got the gist of the Joey saga across, Sal had already taken five delivery orders.

"Are you all right?" Sal asked.

"Me? Yeah. I'm fine."

He gave my face a little slap. "Giovanni, you're a fucking rock. Listen to me. Forget about, Joey. We're gonna get slammed tonight big time. I need you to hustle."

And we did get slammed on account of the rain and all. The storm lasted strong until nine. I did thirty-two deliveries. That's a lot. Actually, it's a Gino's Pizza record. And I finished them all by nine-thirty! Can you believe that? Thirty-two deliveries in four-and-a-half hours. I made one hundred and forty dollars in tips plus twenty-seven in salary. All off the books too. And I loved it. I really loved it. I loved driving through the storm, hydroplaning those big puddles, slicing that thick, heavy rain, jetting along with no visibility. I felt pumped. Pumped! Driving along I pounded the steering wheel when a fast-paced song came on the radio, and, if the radio had no such track, I listened to the intense patter of the rain and the howl of the wind. I felt alive driving in the storm. Those roads—empty, empty, empty—were all mine. They existed for me only. No one else in this piece of shit town even had the balls to jump in their car, let alone befriend the storm, and there I was, cashing in on the whole situation. And when I delivered the food to the people, they seemed so happy to see me. Me, Giovanni Perduto, the deliverer. And I felt happy to see them. After looking at me for just a moment, completely drenched, yet smiling ear to ear, they understood, oh, they felt the spirit, and they all tipped accordingly, with a heavy hand made of monetary justice. You take care of me, kid. I'll take care of you. And when I got back to the base to pick up more deliveries, again I was rewarded with a hero's welcome, this time by Sal, and Vito the cook, and Louie the dishwasher, who was also Sal's second cousin. We were busy there. Sal said he tried to contact Joey, and Marco, the third driver, for help, but he couldn't reach either. A couple of times I came back to the base and even Sal and Luigi ventured out into the storm to deliver aging orders. At this point I must admit, in case you're wondering, I'd be lying if I said I even once thought about old Joey during the course of all them deliveries. For a while the old man didn't even exist. The only thing to me was the storm, and of course, my Maria. But when things slowed down, and the storm cleared up, I felt bad for Joey. Very bad. We all did. He lost his wife. And I felt bad for spying. At the time I didn't realize how close I was to relating with him; yet, still, I shed a tear, as did Sal, when we talked about it later that night, and that's not like Sal at all, to shed a tear, that is.

***

That same night I sat down at the desk in my bedroom and wrote Maria a letter. She planned on coming over at about one in the morning. She was shift-leader and had to close down the restaurant and supervise everyone's side work. Then she had to swing by her parent's house to shower and change. After thinking about Joey's loss, I'd made up my mind. I decided to ask Maria to marry me at once. I had a plan. I'd let her read the letter, get on my knees and pop the question. But first I had to put my love into words for her. I wanted to do it in a creative way, you know what I mean, something unique, for a unique girl. I thought about writing her a story, or a fairy tale, something with a happy ending. Or, if I tried, I could write her a poem. Or maybe even compose my proposal with an acronym sentence made out of her name. Something like: Marriage Always Reeks Innocent Aromas or Marry A Respectable Italian Alchemist. She would've liked that last one. We had an inside joke about turning each other's lead hearts into gold. But what do I know about all that stupid creative crap? Besides, this shit was serious. I let my heart speak. This is what I wrote.

My angel,

Thank you for being in my life. Thank God for creating you. And thank Mother Nature for reflecting your beauty. Every day with you is the first day of the rest of my life. Every day I fall in love with you all over again. I have committed a very deep and personal part of myself, of my soul, to the understanding of your soul. This commitment is forever. I love you. I need you. I love you so much sometimes it burns. I never want to lose you. I want to get old with you. I want to raise your children. I'll be a good daddy. Wait and see. Marry me, baby. Yours forever, Giovanni

***

I hugged Maria at the door. She came inside and sat down on the couch. It was a muggy humid night. The air filled with her flavor, coconuts and amber, sweet to the core. She wore a white tank top, no bra, khaki pants, and white sneakers. Her straight black hair fell past her shoulders and rested on her olive skin. *Madonna,* that brown guinea skin of hers, woof. I don't care. She looks like an angel when she wears white.

She smiled and brushed the hair off her shoulders. Then she took a good look at me and lost her smile.

"What's wrong with your face? Your eye looks swollen. You get into a fight?"

"Joey, from work, he slapped me around a little." I walked over to the couch and sat down beside her. I foolishly thought she would caress me and kiss my swollen pain.

She stood up and walked around the room. "Why would Joey, a sweet, little old man, slap you around? I thought everyone was like family at Gino's."

"We're definitely like family, but Joey's crazy, he flipped. Turns out his wife died. He can't deal. At night, in his house, he sits inside the box he carries deliveries in."

"His wife died? Oh, my god. How sad."

"It's a shame."

"He told you he sits inside a box?"

"I seen him yesterday night. A grown man inside of a box."

She sat beside me on the couch. "You were over his house?"

I can't lie to that girl, so I told her about the mission. "You were spying on him?" She looked like she didn't know who I was. "Gio, you can't do that. You can't do that."

"Listen, Maria, I'm sorry, don't be mad at me." I brushed her cheek and moved her hair away from her face. "He brought that freaking box home with him every night. I wanted to know why." I placed her hand in mine. "Trust me, babe. I regret spying on him. Come on. Don't be mad. I want to give you something. Stay here. I'll go get it."

"I can't believe you sometimes," she said.

I retrieved the words. Maria sat on the couch with her legs crossed. She bit her nails, staring into space. She looked extremely anxious when I came back. I should've seen it coming. I really should've waited for a better mood, a better time, but my dumb ass couldn't. So, I placed the letter on her lap. "Read this. I wrote it for you."

"Gio," she said, ignoring the letter in her lap. "I'm leaving you."

"What?"

I couldn't hear, see or feel nothing. Maybe nothing was all I heard, saw and felt.

"This is hard for me. But I've felt this way for a while. I didn't want to give into the feeling. I always thought it would pass. I thought it would work itself out. It hasn't."

She started to cry. Again, I felt nothing. Not a peaceful, silent nothing, like in them Buddhist books I like to read, but a numb, painful nothing, like in those other stupid philosophy books that confuse the living shit out of me. "I don't understand, baby."

"Sometimes I feel so distant from you. It's as if you're somewhere else. Somewhere no one else could ever be." She looked away. "I think it's time to move on."

My chest heaved and I started to cry.

I couldn't look at her anymore.

I fell. I fell to the floor.

I fell into myself.

I fell into darkness.

***

For three days I confined myself to a box in the basement of my parent's house. The box was big. It used to house a refrigerator my father bought two years ago as a Christmas present for mom. There was more than enough space for me, the four-gallon water jug, a jar to pee in, and some food I'd brought. I had a loaf of Italian bread and some chocolate Nutella, but after two days I decided not to eat until things made sense. Until I understood what happened. Until the pain went away. I'm not good with that kind of pain. You want to slap me around? I can take it. But this pain felt different.

Sitting in the box in the basement, I didn't see any light for three days. It was dark down there and kind of cold. And it smelled stale. I'm not even talking about how I reeked. I smelled. I mean I stunk. I didn't shower in three days. Except for the tears, which didn't stop. After not eating for a day, things began to seem clearer. Maybe it's good to smell your own stink. Maybe it wakes you up. You see, I was thinking I came to an awareness. When spying on Joey I'd been somebody I didn't recognize. Somebody I didn't know I could be. Yet for some reason I didn't feel guilty. Maybe I should've, I'm not sure. I saw it like this. I'm this mind and body, the good with the bad, and I don't have any other choice, right? Who I am will always get in the way of me being who I want to be, but hey, I have to meet my future, even if it meant without Maria? I didn't really know the answer. Maybe I just felt hunger pains.

That's about the time I heard the basement door open. Somebody turned the light on and walked downstairs. Was it my parents? Maria? I couldn't see. Three days in the dark. My eyes burned from the light. I gently rubbed them and the first thing I noticed when my eyes adjusted to the light was a smiling face looking down on me.

"Joey," I said, "what are you doing?"

"It smells down here," he said. The old man looked good. He looked healthy. I felt happy to see him. He told me how everyone wondered about my whereabouts. How they missed me at work. He told me Maria went to him because she was also worried. She wanted to see me. He extended his hand. "Why don't you come out of the box?"

"Joe, I'm sorry I spied on you like that."

"*A tutto c'è rimedio, fuorchè alla morte.* There's a cure for everything, except death." He kept his hand extended. "Gio, the world is crazy as it is. And sometimes it gets so foggy you don't know what to do. Things happen. You don't see them coming."

I wiped my eyes. Enough was enough.

I felt like the young fool that I am.

"I'm hungry, Joey."

"Come on. The box isn't the answer for you, son."

I took his hand and climbed out.

MONROE
Miami, Florida, 2002

On the southern edge of Little Haiti at Churchill's, a bar representing the cradle of alternative culture in Miami, three cop cars, blue and red flashing deep in the night, and a Miami-Dade ambulance idled. There. On the way to Jackson Memorial and then county prison. Right there. Look. James Monroe lay on a stretcher. A bloody pulp.

Monroe was a big guy, athletic. He played baseball. A southpaw. Monroe was good too. In Little League no one could hit him. In high school he made All-State in Kentucky. *USA Today* ran a feature on him. Now he lay on a stretcher, a bloody mess.

All his life Monroe dreamt of hurling for the Atlanta Braves. To have his name in that All-Star rotation. Maddux, Smoltz, Glavine, Monroe. He drifted to sleep most nights dreaming of his smiling face in the left-hand corner of ESPN's *Sportscenter*.

Coaches, friends, and family enabled his dreams: *You're going to be a star, Monroe.* Monroe almost made it. He pitched for the Miami Hurricanes, second man in the rotation, as a freshman. James Monroe was an integral part of the Miami Hurricanes baseball team for two seasons. Both years the teams ranked in the top-ten of the *Associated Press* and *Sporting News* polls. Then Monroe blew out his arm. Tore his rotator cuff in a way in which he could never pitch again.

Monroe *was* a shooting star.

Predictably, Monroe turned to drugs. He had a problem with GHB. A big problem. GHB, gamma hydroxybutyrate, was sold over-the-counter until 1990. Athletes used it to raise growth hormone levels and reduce body fat. It had severe side effects and was soon classified as a schedule II drug. GHB appears as an odorless liquid, slightly salty to the taste. It's served in teaspoons and bottle caps. At lower doses, GHB has a euphoric effect similar to alcohol; higher doses will make the user dizzy and sleepy; overdoses can result in a temporary coma and sometimes death. Always something.

At first Monroe used GHB *only* to work out. He copped it from a homeboy, Clifton, the catcher on his squad, and a brother at Kappa Sigma. The brothers used to throw down GHB at frat parties. On a couple of occasions, women woke up next to Monroe unsure how. But Jimmy Monroe wasn't like that. Not at all. He didn't know how the girls wound up next to him either. No one cared. They were happy to lay with Monroe—cause James Monroe was somebody on campus, and James Monroe was going to be a star. If *only* they could've seen him at Churchill's—a bloody, pulpy mess.

Everyone's a couple of steps from the street. The steps can fall like dominos. Miami may be lined with beautiful palm trees, and the air filled with a sea breeze, but the streets are merciless. In the Miami streets, you're on your own; worst of all, no one cares.

Within one year of blowing out his arm, Monroe found himself arrested for possession of GHB outside the popular nightclub Level on South Beach. Consequently, he was also expelled from the University of Miami, his full ride scholarship pulled due to legal troubles and academic failings. Worst of all, Monroe was cut off from his family.

Monroe hailed from a conservative family in Kentucky. The Monroe's of Louisville. Society folk. The Monroe's among the top ten non-corporate donors to the Kentucky Republican Party. Their money came from the thoroughbred horse industry. They bred horses, owned a Kentucky Derby winning stud on their farm. Big deal. Yet his family refused to lift a finger unless he moved back to Kentucky. Monroe wasn't giving up on Miami. For some, Miami is not an easy city to leave.

As it turned out, Miami gave up on Monroe.

His brothers at Kappa Sigma tried to help him out.

They set up an intervention hoping to convince Monroe to check into rehab. At the frat house they even hung a giant banner: Get Help Buddy. No one caught the irony.

After expulsion, a few brothers let him crash at their pads. But the bridges burned quickly when jewelry, electronics and game consuls began to turn up missing. At the U of M, it wasn't long before the consensus on James Monroe went like this: *fuck him bro.*

Monroe became homeless. He used to have soft skin, showering every day with Dove soap. After only a month the Miami sun transformed his skin into a hard leathery brown. Monroe began to resemble a baseball glove. The young man lost all direction.

And Monroe went way beyond GHB. He wandered around Miami spare changing money to get high off of five-dollar crack rocks he picked up in Overtown under the bridge of Interstate 95. The ex-star athlete bathed once a week, sometimes in the fountain at the Miami Beach Holocaust Memorial, sometimes he bathed in a canal.

One muggy humid Tuesday night, Monroe ventured to Churchill's to see a show. He had been kicking it with this gutterpunk from Missouri. Sarah, from Joplin, she had a system for abusing welfare, emergency homeless funds and food stamps acquired across multiple counties. Instant cash. The computers not advanced enough to catch the fraud. Bureaucracy. They met at a "pill mill" buried in Biscayne Park. Monroe and the gutterpunk had one hobby in common: Oxycontin. They rolled together, bender after bender, strip mall "pill mill" after strip mall "pill mill." She mailed Oxy's back to Missouri for money. And he protected her. Monroe and that left hook.

On that muggy Tuesday night in Little Haiti, Sarah the gutterpunk from Joplin, Missouri found some trick and stranded Monroe at Churchill's. Whatever, end of a bender. Monroe didn't trust her anyway. Jimmy Monroe trusted no one.

Monroe felt so tired he crawled inside the double-decker bus at Churchill's and fell asleep. The red bus, painted like the flag of England, was a Churchill's landmark. It lay immobile in a dirt lot across the street from the pub. Sometimes Monroe slept in it. The owner of Churchill's was okay with Monroe sleeping in the bus. He followed college baseball. Felt he owed it to Monroe and the city of Miami. The city could be more loyal than one might think, especially to those who lasted and lingered, broken by its tropics.

So, it went for many weeks. Monroe wandered around the city during the day then made his way back to the bus as the moon rose. At night he hung with kids in the parking lot outside the bus, drinking beers; he sang along with acoustic guitars; he tried busting rhymes in hip-hop ciphers. He was liked, for the most part. Until he blew a fuse.

Churchill's hosted a night for everything. Monday jazz in the front, spoken word in the back. Tuesday hip hop. Wednesday ladies wrestling night. Thursday punk rock.

It was a crowded Wednesday. Two women slopping around a ring filled with mud and cherries. The match almost over and the girls naked. Monroe bum rushed the ring and began wrestling the girls. He ripped off his shirt. Utter chaos and nonsense.

Monroe took the bouncer's jabs, *body-blow*, he lost his breath, his stomach caved in, he wasn't going to be on his feet for much longer, *upper-cut*, he crumbled, *he's down for the count*; Monroe fell to the ground like Glass Joe in that old *Punch Out* game.

He wound up in jail. Already on probation his bail was set at $100,000. Luckily, and almost immediately regrettably, his family in Kentucky posted it. Within a week Monroe skipped bail and left Florida for New Orleans. Monroe's happen every other day in Miami. And Miami, stifling, ruthless Miami. Miami goes on, not giving two shits.

REAL EYES
Hollywood, Florida, 2002

Emily woke up and couldn't see.

She felt fine the previous night reading in bed. In the morning, she couldn't open her eyes and felt blinded with pain.

"Help me, Jake. Help me," she yelled.

Jake meandered about the kitchen cooking an omelet. He planned to surprise Emily with breakfast in bed. It was the morning of her twenty-fifth birthday and Jake had plans: breakfast in bed, a trip to the gardens, a picnic at the beach, a sunset stroll, fondue dinner, and then regional theatre. Jake thought he had good plans until the screams came and scared the romance out of him. The screams rang loud.

He ran towards the bedroom.

Along the way, Jake stubbed his toe on the chair at the dining room table in between the kitchen and the hallway. He stumbled into the hallway wall, knocking down a hanging print of Dali's *Hallucinogenic Toreador*. And then he burst into the bedroom.

"What's wrong, baby?"

"I can't see." She sat on the bed, on her knees, her arms out in front of her, swatting the air. "It hurts. Oh my God—"

Jake jumped on the bed and grabbed her hands.

"It's okay. It's all right. Calm down."

"Oh my God!"

"Can you open your eyes?"

"I can't. They burn—"

Jake didn't know what to do. He stroked her hair.

"It still hurts with them closed?"

She nodded. "It feels heavy, with pressure. Oh my God—"

"Keep them closed. They're swollen. I'll go get some ice."

"Help me, God, oh my God, h-e-l-l-l-l," she moaned. Her pain hung in the air. Jake was conditioned, if something looked swollen, or burned, you iced it down, so he bolted towards the kitchen. As he ran down the hallway, his nostrils became bombarded with the aroma of a burnt egg. Soon his eyes were stung by a gray omelet vapor. The skillet sat under a high flame sizzling and through the foggy fume he reached for the pan. Jake grabbed the griddle without protection and charred his right hand on the radiating pan and in a flash of pain his burning fingers turned numb. The pan fell on the floor with a resounding *twang*, the sound reverberating into the annoying blare of the smoke alarm that started to blast. Jake ran to the sink and doused his burns with water.

"Help me, Jacob. H-e-l-l-l-p."

Her shrieks hung in the air; their deep tone penetrated the high pitch of the smoke alarm, like a bass in Halloween's orchestra.

Inside the freezer lay an old tan ice pack. Jake unscrewed the top and filled it with two trays of ice cubes. Some of the ice sailed across the kitchen as he tried to get it out. The alarm didn't stop ringing. It hung high on the wall near the front door of the living room. Jake grabbed a chair from the dining room table and yanked the alarm off the wall. Then he jumped off the seat, landing awkwardly on his left ankle. Feeling a slight hobble, he trekked into the kitchen, snatched the ice pack and darted back into the bedroom.

Emily sat at the foot of the bed her feet planted on the ground. Her head turned down; her strawberry curls frazzled chaos. Emily covered her eyes. Jake sat down next to his partner and brushed the hair away from her face. He gently rubbed her head.

"Here." He handed over the ice pack.

She held the ice to her face.

"There's something seriously wrong," she said.

"We're going to the ER."

They threw on some clothes. He grabbed the car keys.

It was cold, foggy and gray outside, with no sign of the sun.

"My eyes are killing me," she said.

They descended the many steps of their complex. Then jumped in the Civic and took off. Emily looked antsy during the ride to the ER. She covered her eyes with her palms while rubbing her temples with nervous fingers. She gave up on the icepack. Jake asked if a chemical or acid landed in her eye. Maybe something lodged in there. That would've made sense. She said no. She said she woke up because of a nasty nightmare. When she woke up, she had an incredible headache and then finally her eyes shut down.

They exploded through the sliding doors into the waiting room.

"We have an emergency," Jake yelled.

Within two minutes Emily was whisked away. They wouldn't let Jake in. A nurse told him to sit in the waiting room. As soon as they knew something he'd hear about it. He moved the car away from the hospital entrance and paced outside. In the waiting room, where Jake didn't want to be, he looked shaky with jitters and pulled on his hair.

It thundered outside.

"Sounds like a storm," an old man remarked. He was a big man with white in his hair. He sat next to Jake gripping a cane. It thundered again. "Storm's coming."

"It'll be all right," Jake said.

"Do you realize?"

"Realize what?" Jake asked.

They continued to wait, in silence, until Jake hobbled over to the concession stand and purchased a bottle of water. He jerked around from the machine, not noticing the delivery guy carrying a bouquet of roses. The glass vase flew out of his hands and shattered on the floor. Water trickled down the waiting room hall. Jake helped the delivery guy gather up the roses—the man wore a red shirt that said Victor's Flowers—and Jake cut his middle finger, the same hand that was earlier burned, on the thorns.

"I'm so clumsy," he said, sucking his bloody finger with one hand, digging into his pockets for a ten-dollar bill with the other. "Here, take this, for your trouble."

"No trouble," the delivery guy said, taking the ten. "Accidents happen."

A janitor strolled over and cleaned up the mess.

Jake continued to wait.

After two hours, a doctor led him into a consulting room.

Judging by the symptoms Emily mentioned while conscious—while conscious—*the elevated eye pressure, the severe eye pain, it may be acute closed angle glaucoma.* Emily's too young to have glaucoma. No? *Age is the most significant risk factor, and closed angle glaucoma is rare, but it can hit suddenly.* Doctor, give it to me straight. *Most likely it's a headache. Both sinus and tension headaches can cause eye pain and pressure. Headaches are like fingerprints, no two are alike. They're difficult to diagnose.*

A headache?

Jake wanted to see Emily. He wanted to reach out his hands and touch her, hopefully with a soothing effect, maybe making her pain subside, if only for a moment.

The doctor said they injected her eyes with lidocaine, to ease the discomfort. She'd temporarily passed out but was conscious again. He had a nurse lead Jake to her.

When he saw her, he said, "Oh my god."

"Jake. Is that you, Jake?"

She leaned up in bed and reached her hands out in front of her.

Tender was the embrace when their hands met.

"It's me. It's me, baby."

Over Emily's eyes were six patches, three attached to each lid. The three patches fixed over each eye were fastened by four pieces of surgical tape, extending from her forehead to her cheek. The doctor entered the room. He explained that three patches over each eye were necessary to create enough bulk to secure the eyelid.

"We don't want her to see."

Jake kneeled on the floor, still holding Emily's hands.

"Some birthday, huh?"

"It's dark, Jake."

"You'll be all right."

"It doesn't feel all right." She sighed. "Not now."

"This is only temporary," Jake said. "Try not to worry. I love you so much."

He closed his eyes and kept them closed.

SUNNY DELIGHT
In memoriam
Coconut Grove, Miami, 2006

Rafael de la Roche was a man of the arts. A director of the theater. An aesthete. Art for art's sake—the motto he barked at actors when they self-righteously questioned their own motivation for portraying a character of ill taste.

Rafael owned a venue in Coconut Grove called The Black Box. A relatively small theater with a hundred seats. The Black Box could be considered a success—the company performed many plays that went on to win Carbonell's, the South Florida equivalent of a Tony Award. They performed established classics, like its annual December production of *A Christmas Carol,* as well as Southeast Premieres and even World Premiers, many of which original works by local playwrights. In fact, one such original production went on to win a Pulitzer Prize in Drama. Notwithstanding merit, but also by happenstance, the house playwright was awarded the prize in a year when the competition consisted of a script written by a three-time winner and another about homosexuality—a theme rewarded the previous year by the committee.

Regardless, with theater goers Rafael had a generous habit of cordiality. Before every performance he would meet and greet each patron at the front door with a smile and a handshake. Thanks to Rafael the patrons of The Black Box always felt at home, and they expressed their comfort through loyalty to the theater and donations. Ironically, even though the theater had a solid subscription base, as is the case with many organizations within the arts, it struggled financially. Despite donors and grants, hey, art for art's sake, right? But one year in particular the struggling theater reached a point of no return. The country was in the seventh year of a conservative regime and funding from the usual national endowments was at a bare minimum, with all federal monies being directed away from the arts and allocated to the pursuit of defense. The theater, despite reducing its season from the usual six productions to five, was for the first time in its twenty-eight-year history in serious jeopardy of going fiscally bankrupt.

And then, Vincent D'nuzzio walked through the door.

He arrived at the theater alone. Judging from his girth, greasy hair, and pointy shoes, Rafael concluded he was neither a critic nor a diehard patron of the arts. In fact, D'nuzzio was there to see Dora Vain, a girl he'd met two nights prior moonlighting at Scarletts — the strip club in Hallandale off of I 95. Dora had an ensemble role in The Black Box's production at the time, *Mosshead*, a play written by a FIU grad student.

Dora invited D'nuzzio to come see her perform *Mosshead* at the Black Box. The Italian, in town from Tampa for a week, took the invitation to be a euphemism for oral sex. He sat in the back row and listened to Rafael de la Roche introduce the play. As Rafael solicited the scarce theater crowd for subscriptions a dark plot hatched in D'nuzzio's mind. His partners in Tampa were looking for a desperate business in Miami to wash illicit money. D'nuzzio's current mission in Miami was twofold: complete the latest transaction with the Peruvian contact and then find a way to launder their money.

D'nuzzio walked out of the show halfway through. *No broad's worth sittin true dis*. On his way out, in the lobby, he ran into Rafael. *Jus the man I was lookin for*. "Yo."

"Yes," Rafael said, despondent.

"Can I talk to you bout something?"

D'nuzzio was straightforward. He'd give the theater a donation of a hundred thousand dollars in cash, if and only if, the theater wrote checks for eighty thousand to wherever and whoever they were told to. No questions asked. If it went simple, they'd do it five times a year. If it didn't go simple, well, it wouldn't be so simple for Rafael.

Rafael sighed. But he didn't say no.

He didn't say yes. But he didn't say no.

He lived in Miami. The offer not *too* surprising.

D'nuzzio slid him a card. "Think about it."

Rafael knew a hundred thousand dollars a year could save the theater. But he wasn't a criminal. A man of culture, what did he know about crime? He was a man of art. He didn't do business with thugs. *I directed an original Pulitzer Prize winning play*. But he needed the money. The Endowment canceled grants. He couldn't lose his theater.

He thought about it. Slept on it.

The show must go on. He decided on it.

Over time, Rafael de la Roche became less and less curious about the business of D'nuzzio and his Tampa partners. He would have bet his fledgling theater they were dealing in drugs, yet for some reason that didn't bother him; around artists his whole life, over time a certain contempt arose in Rafael with regards to the criminalization of drugs.

He did what he was told and wrote the checks. He wrote the checks for two years, devising a way to write it all off under suspicious Schedule C1 tax categories.

When it went down with the FBI, he no longer took an apathetic stance to the American legal system, and he learned D'nuzzio didn't deal drugs. He was a smuggler.

D'nuzzio, it turned out, was a leading player in an animal smuggling ring that caught the attention of the Feds. A manager of the zoo at Busch Gardens secretly bred endangered monkeys and giraffes, both priceless. A groom at the zoo gave the animals to D'nuzzio, who then drove down to Miami and sold them to a Peruvian named Gustavo.

Gustavo worked in Lima for a wealthy American ex-patriot, a San Francisco tekkie, a dot-commer who had the perspective to take the money and run while the getting was good. The FBI didn't want the ex-patriot. The Feds, in cooperation with the Miami-Dade police department, wanted D'nuzzio. D'nuzzio was linked to the Trafficante crime family in Tampa. The officer's toes tingled at a chance to bust the mob, especially because it was an election year.

But they had nothing on D'nuzzio.

All they had was Rafael.

Because of his relationship with D'nuzzio, no matter how tepid the nature, the Feds were ready to slap Rafael's file with the notorious label of organized crime. With the label came the dreaded attachment of the Racketeer Influenced and Corrupt Organizations Act. RICO, along with strict prison sentencing, forced forfeiture of any interest, property, or holding acquired or maintained in violation of the act.

For Rafael, it meant losing the theater. He had a real problem. If he ratted on D'nuzzio, his life would be worthless. If he didn't rat, what was there to look forward to without his theater? The days went by and Rafael didn't know what to do.

In his happiest days, when the theater received good reviews, Rafael walked from his West Avenue apartment down Lincoln Road feeling satisfied. He felt like the faces of the models he passed, lovely. But now, he thought about extinction; his imagination always saved him from fearing death. But now, the idea of oblivion seemed novel.

It could be a way out. A dramatic tragedy.

After doing extensive research on the internet, he came upon a recipe for a certain solution. At his South Beach apartment, with the efficiency of a trained chemist, he produced the said solution and mixed it into a quart of Sunny Delight orange juice.

It was a beautiful day and there was at least one hour of sunlight left in the sky. His direction turned westward. He drove off the beach, west on 395, west on 836, west, west, west, until he reached the edge of the Everglades. Sipping Sunny Delight, he parked his car and ventured to a trail that ran along the edge of the Everglades. *The show must go on.* Soon his drink emptied. The sun setting, a beautiful sight. The sky like the mixed palette of a divine painter. He dropped to his knees.

The show...must...go...

When the Miami-Dade police officers found the body nine days later it was missing a leg, an arm, and its head. Federal agents were called in and they suspected D'nuzzio of the dismembering—thanks to an autopsy the cause of death was eventually ruled suicide by poison and the missing appendages were attributed to a hungry alligator.

MASSAGE PARLOR
North Miami. Florida, 1998

You pick up the phone and dial the spa ad you clipped from *The Herald* sports pages. The spa is near work. "How much for a massage?" you ask. The answer is $30 for a half-hour, $50 for an hour, plus tip. No appointment necessary. You go during lunch.

The parlor, off of Biscayne Boulevard, is nestled in the corner of a strip mall, next to a pet supermarket and a pizzeria. The red sign above the parlor is simple and to the point: MASSAGE. It's raining outside and you're still in the car. The windshield wipers are loud and need to be replaced. *You're stalling. You scared?* The front door is glass. You walk inside, a bell rings. You don't notice the brown-haired man with the stubble. You don't see him, sitting, waiting, reading *The Daily Racing Form*. You're drawn to the young Asian behind the desk. You want a half-hour session.

The Asian asks for 30 bucks. You don't realize you can pick the masseuse. You don't understand you can send the girl back if you don't like the way she looks. You don't know anything. You're a dog on a leash as the Asian girl leads you to room number one. Why was the stubble-faced man sitting, waiting, reading? "Undress, lie on table. Cover up," she tells you, pointing to a washcloth. "Girl be in shortly." The white room feels sterile to you, impersonal, cold, although a candle is burning. This place reminds you of the nurse's office at elementary school, a place you'd sometimes land when they served sloppy joes. In the room, there's a radio, towel, chair. There's a massage table—blue leather—in the middle of the room. A washcloth sits on top of it.

You get naked, leaving your clothes on the chair, climbing aboard the table. You lie on your stomach, place the white washcloth over your ass and wait. You're nervous.

No, I'm not. Yes, you are.

The door opens.

"Hello." A voice, soft, but faceless. *Is she big is she cute is she Asian is she white?* You can't see, you're face down on the massage table. Whoever she is, she's lit sandalwood incense and put on New Age music. "I'm Amethyst," she says, walking to where you can see her. Amethyst is beautiful—a tight bodied, straight-haired, African American young woman with sparkling black eyes.

You didn't expect her to be beautiful.

Amethyst pours baby oil in her hands and begins to gently rub your back and shoulders. You relax. You're a stick of melting butter. For fifteen minutes, you're *butter*.

You learn things about Amethyst. She grew up in Atlanta. She's nineteen, studying visual arts at the local community college, and dating a thirty-four-year-old Social Studies teacher. He's married. Amethyst massages your lower back, very slowly. She's gentler than your girlfriend. She throws the towel off your ass and rubs your sciatic. You learn she's worked at the parlor for two weeks. She doesn't know her dad. She's got Native American in her blood and that's why her hair is straight. "Turn over," she says. "I'm going to work on your front."

"Is $40 a good tip?" you ask, your time is almost up.

"Forty's fine," she says.

Her hands are soft, but strong. Her hands could build, they could build. They could build a building, a big building. The baby oil does it. Then it comes: time's up.

The massage is over. Amethyst exits the room.

Are you supposed to feel dirty? Because you don't. You clean up with the towel, dress and leave the parlor a new man.

CRUISE TO NOWHERE
Downtown Miami, 2004

Outside on the top deck the air smells like exhaust as the *Casino Princesa* purrs at its Bayside port. The ship embarks, sailing along the inlet away from Downtown. The vessel passes million-dollar homes on Hibiscus and Palm Island. A flock of pelicans soar by. A Colombian with a video camera strikes up conversation. He's in town picking up parts for his air-conditioning business back home. "Your city is beautiful," he says, in broken English, spitting in your face, "not like Bogota. This boat. Everything so nice." There are four decks, casinos on the first two, and a cafeteria on the third. The decor inside the ship is a 70's mod, the carpet right out of *Fear and Loathing in Las Vegas*.

In the casino an eclectic group of Miamians perch themselves about waiting for the action to start upon entering international waters. The starring players in this drama are mainly seniors: African-American, Jewish, and Cuban couples. The cast also includes degenerate men — it appears they haven't shaved in a week, giving off the impression they came to the cruise straight from Dania Jai Alai. To counter the boys, a group of desperado women swivel in seats in front of the slots. They're smoking cigarettes. Pall Malls. Virginia Slims. There are thirty-something lawyers fresh off of work from Brickell offices, swilling beer, big guts bulging over five hundred-dollar suits. There is a group of males under thirty all wearing sports jerseys. And a single Latino sits next to a slot machine, he's staring out the window, waiting, banging on a plastic bin like a drum.

"The *Princesa* has reached international waters. Let the casino begin," a voice says over the intercom. The slots light up, bells ring, coins drop — *bink dink chink* — chips rustle. Y*awwrrr*, international waters. Press your luck, Miami. No whammy, no whammy.

A degenerate sits down in the empty seat next to you at the blackjack table. The first hand he plays he draws an ace and a king — it would've been *your* ace and *your* king — the bastard. Can you forgive him? You try but can't. He's wearing a Texas Tuxedo, denim shirt, denim pants, hails from Hialeah he says. You head outside.

The excursion is five hours long. Looking east at the ocean appears ominous, the sea dark, black and expansive. You're slightly scared. Looking west, relief, the coastline a secure reminder where the cars are parked. You smoke, thinking of the radio advertisement with the catchy jingle: *Casino Princesa—it's-your-kind-of-party*. Your cigarette is flicked over the railing. It lands on the canvas cover of a lifeboat and starts to burn a hole. You head inside. Near the craps table, the under thirty males in sports jerseys turn out to be NFL football players, one an ex-Hurricane and a New York Giant. They're talking about the free shit they get from sponsors. Back at blackjack Texas Tuxedo redeems himself by tossing an old Cuban a five-dollar chip. The senior goes on a streak and gives Texas Tuxedo back his loan, plus a chip interest.

They both tip the dealer.

"Thiss is the mosst boring five hours I've ever ssspent," someone spits in your ear. It's the Colombian. He looks haggard, clutching a bottle of water. You're doubling down on sevens, double fisted with 7 & sevens. "Gambling cruise, you have to gamble."

Waitresses wander around. "Cocktails, cocktails."

At exactly eleven-thirty the casino and bar shut down and the big boat heads back to port. There's one more hour before the *Princesa* unleashes its two hundred patrons back on the city. It's an hour when you want something to happen, anything—a drunk falling overboard, a manatee caught in the rudder. All that's left are memories of splitting aces, playing ten the hard way, and laying it all on thirty-six red.

ARE YOU HUNGRY?

ACKNOWLEDGEMENTS

This tiny book was a long time in the making. Many stories were published in a variety of publications, including The Miami Herald, Miami New Times, Mary, a Literary Quarterly, where "The Box" was awarded a prize in short fiction and Carve, where "Looking for Margarita" received their Raymond Carver Award.

Thank you to the editors who published my work, with an emphasis on Brett O'Bourke and the late Michael Rothenberg, who was a heck of a poet. Thank you, Amanda, and Johnny, Joanna and the Akashic Team who bounced this around.

Big shout out to my entire FIU writing community, with an emphasis on Campbell McGrath, John Dufresne and Lynne Barrett. Thank you to all of my students and colleagues at Miami Dade College and to the Miami literary community at large. Thank you of course to my friends and readers who pushed me to get this book out, including Gina, Omar, Yousi, and David Rolland.

Much love to my family, both chosen, and to whom are stuck with me.

Thank you, thank you, thank you.

ABOUT THE AUTHOR

J. J. Colagrande is the author of *Headz, Reduce Heat Continue to Boil* and *Decò 2.0*.
He lives in Miami and works as a Professor at Miami Dade College.